About the author

Liam Randles lives on the Wirral with his partner Katie, stepdaughter Isla, and a Chihuahua named Elvis. *The Heat of the Summer* is his first published novel.

> Dear Loz,
> Thanks for coming to the launch and supporting me! It's greatly appreciated!
> Lots of love,
> Liam x

The Heat of the Summer

Liam Randles

Published by Armley Press, 2022
ISBN 978-1-9160165-6-9

© Liam Randles

Copy editing: Gareth Pugh & John Lake
Cover design: Mick Lake
Cover photo: Jeremy Bishop @unsplash
Typesetting: Ian Dobson
Production: Mick McCann

Printed by Lightning Source

This is a work of fiction. Any resemblance to persons living or dead, or events past or present, is entirely coincidental.

To my parents, my partner Katie, and Isla Harrison. Thank you for all the love, support and encouragement.

'I come no enemy, but to set free
From out this dark and dismal house of pain.'
– John Milton, *Paradise Lost*

1

"A week away from reality."
　　Jordan raises his shot glass. The rest of us follow his lead.
　　"A week away from reality," we all chime.
　　A week away from reality. No family stuff. No part-time job. Put the anxieties over starting university in September to one side. Same with the worries over keeping in touch with everybody. My virginity. Thoughts about the future. A career. Settling down. Getting a mortgage. Health. Wealth. Happiness. The state of the world and how it always seems to get worse every time I check Twitter. The imminent arrival of environmental catastrophe or nuclear war or another pandemic. The prevalence of terrorism. The rise of the far right. Geopolitical shite. The economy going down the toilet. The fact that the clock is turning back towards a time that felt less safe, less enlightened. Back to an altogether scarier place. And how everyone feels completely powerless to stop it happening.
　　All of it, every little bit of it can be put on ice for a week. Because I'm sure it will be waiting for me when I return home.
　　The four of us are getting away from our worries for a week. Four friends on our first lads' holiday together.

―

We throw back the contents of our shot glasses. A gloopy red liquid that tastes like cinnamon and smells like burning. We slam the glasses down hard against the table.
　　Each of us reacts the same way. A dry retch. A choke for air.
　　The initial unpleasantness quickly subsides. We seem to forget it the moment it slops down our gullets. Knowing looks form across our faces. Goofy grins. Goofy laughs.
　　We're all on the same wavelength. We're all after a good time.

―

The Heat of the Summer

The airport bar. Early morning.
I'm pissed. I don't mind admitting it. The air feels fuzzy. Stifling. Almost as if my head is working on a delayed reaction. Everything takes longer to process. Everything everyone says is inexplicably funny.

I feel my worries recede. An image pops into my head of a tranquil sea reflecting a cloudless sky, a vivid orange sun hanging high casting its rays across the water's surface.

I look around the bar. A few businessmen in expensive suits are clutching tumblers of whiskey on the rocks, talking loudly in the shadow of an LCD TV tuned in to a news channel depicting some atrocity in the Middle East. There are the usual assorted groups of middle-aged men and middle-aged women, stag and hen parties, married couples, kids running around as though feral. A young woman in her early twenties is alone at a table in front of a half-drunk glass of white wine. A vacant expression is etched on her face. She stares dead-eyed straight ahead beyond our table and right out of the bar towards the departure lounge. Her hair is pulled together in a messy ponytail. She runs her fingers up and down the stem of the wine glass.

The conversation at the table disintegrates into a low buzz. Everyone around me is in hysterics. It feels like a slow-motion shot in a film. The thought stirs that maybe the joke is at my expense. Maybe at my virginity. My attention remains on the sad-looking woman while I take a few more mouthfuls of beer, hoping that the conversation will naturally change course.

Maybe it will stop if I remain silent. Stay completely still.

I sometimes wish I could blend into my surroundings and disappear.

―

Ewan replies to something that Caleb has said. It sets Jordan off. He bangs a meaty fist against the table top in response. The drinks ripple. Just like that famous scene from Jurassic Park.

The Heat of the Summer

I glance around the bar while this goes on. But I find that my stare always returns to the sad-looking young woman with the glass of wine.

—

There's a persistent din in my ears. A hammering noise.

I'm dragged from my thoughts. My skin pricks at the realisation that the noise is coming from Jordan. His eyes are fixed on me as I make out my name being repeated over and over.

"What?" I respond.

"Are you hoping to lose your V-plates on this trip or what, kid?" he asks me through a wry smile.

Ewan and Caleb both howl.

I pretend I haven't heard anything. I switch my attention back to the woman with the glass of wine at this exact moment. She notices my stare this time and transmits a pained smile that makes me feel uncomfortable so I abruptly look away. I glance over my shoulder at the hordes crisscrossing the terminal floor. And then out of the giant floor-to-ceiling windows where a plane leaves the runway and soars into a moody grey sky.

—

Ready for take-off.

I fidget in my seat.

I've always hated flying. I remember once flying home with my parents from a summer holiday in Spain. Years before they split up. Even before Ruby was born. I must have been six at the time. Maybe seven. But it's a memory as clear as the picture on an IMAX cinema screen, regardless.

I was in the middle seat between my parents. The flight attendants strode up and down the aisle checking each passenger's seat belt was fastened correctly as they shut the overhead bins.

The pilot said something through the intercom. His voice was muffled.

Mum was drunk. She's another terrible flier. I suspect that her worries have shaped my own anxieties. She had a few gin

The Heat of the Summer

and tonics before the flight. I remember she squeezed my hand on take-off. She clutched it so tight that the colour drained quickly and it felt as though my fingers were about to break. I winced and my mother noticed this and bowed her head and kissed me hard on the cheek and slurred how much she loved me through a sloppy smile. The pain in my hand settled into a dull throb with the plane's ascent and I turned my head towards my father, who seemed preoccupied gazing out of the window. He was lost in his thoughts. Like my mother and I didn't exist.

The turbulence started soon after take-off. The whole plane shook.

I was scared. Even then it felt like fear in its purest form. It's something that has stayed with me all this time because whenever I had been scared up until that point, my parents had always calmed me down. There was no danger they could not dispel. Monsters under the bed. Weird shapes in the dark. The bogeyman would always be banished by a warm hug and some kind, soothing words. A soft kiss would inevitably follow. Their mere presence was more than enough to reassure me that nothing bad could happen.

But it was different this time. I remember glancing right and then left as the plane shuddered in mid-air. My mother grabbed my hand even tighter than before and closed her eyes and started muttering stuff under her breath. She was saying a prayer or having a conversation with herself or something. Her face whitened, turned the same colour as my hand. I became worried watching her. I tried to pull away, but the force she exerted was almost superhuman. I winced and shrieked in the hope that the noise would snap her out of it, but it failed to attract a response.

Dad was similarly absent. I watched him take out some pills from the inside of his jacket pocket and then knock them back with a gulp of bottled water. He turned his shoulders away from me and then forced his eyes shut and did not open them again for the remainder of the flight.

Panic spread through the plane. Anguished cries echoed with every abrupt jerk and wild bounce. A baby's wail came from somewhere behind me. An elderly woman across the aisle had to be promised that everything was okay by a stewardess. The pilot addressed the passengers at some point to plead for calm, but it only induced a greater level of anxiety. I remember the man in the seat behind me repeatedly crying out to God.

It was probably the first time I ever felt alone. The first time I felt I could not rely on my parents. The only thing I could compare it to was when I lost my mother in a supermarket a few years previously. The fear was every bit as acute, every bit as consuming. But I can remember how that subsided the instant my mother clasped my hand when we were reunited. All it took for that to happen was a message over the PA after I told a shelf stacker that I was lost. I remember Mum smiled at me and promised that she would never let me out of her sight again. She said she would always be there for me whenever I needed her.

—

The memory of that flight has come back to me on every occasion I've flown since. I close my eyes and see it clearly.

My breathing escalates. It feels like my chest is being compressed in a vice. A bead of sweat drips from my brow.

Caleb is next to me. I feel him shuffle to reach inside his pocket. He nudges me in the ribs, prompting me to open my eyes.

I tune back into my surroundings. He rattles a plastic pot of pills.

"Want one?" he asks.

"What are they?"

"Magic beans," he says. "They'll help your nerves. My mum swears by them."

I stay silent.

"Trust me, Luke," he adds. "They'll take the edge off."

"I've had a drink, mate."

The Heat of the Summer

Caleb rolls his eyes. "You're not exactly a fucking rock star, bud. Nothing bad is going to happen. Stop being such a fucking baby all the time, okay?"

I glance around. Ewan is asleep in the window seat. Jordan is across the aisle in conversation with some girls who look around the same age as us. I listen in to hear him ask the girls where they are staying. The crackle of the intercom drowns out their response, along with a few more exchanges. Laughter breaks during a rare moment of quiet. One of the girls reminds the other of a checklist they drew up when the holiday was booked. Boys took top spot on their to-do list. The cackle this elicits from Jordan cuts through me.

I give Caleb my hand. He breaks a tablet in two and places the marginally bigger half in my palm.

"How about a half, Luke? For your first time. Wouldn't want you becoming an addict, would we?"

Caleb then hands me a half-drunk bottle of Coke that's been mixed with some duty-free vodka. I throw back the pill and take a swallow of the drink without another thought entering my head.

The plane circles the runway before gradually picking up speed. The engine whirs.

I clasp my hands around the back of my head and lean back in my seat and shut my eyes. I feel myself grow tired. I allow a deep sleep to envelop me, secure in the knowledge that I'm only a couple of hours from being as far away from reality as can be imagined.

2

The half-full coach taking us to the hotel journeys along hazardous terrain. It crawls along a narrow road forged into the side of a dusty orange rock face with a low barrier of rusty iron bollards and chicken wire edging a drop of a hundred feet or more. The road itself is cut up and littered with potholes, bumps and grooves. The coach's suspension jerks. Each uncomfortable bounce prompts a whopping cheer from most of the passengers on board, like we're on some rickety fairground ride.

And, strangely, I find that none of this bothers me one little bit. Neither does the fact that I can barely remember the flight or stepping through passport control or picking up my case from the baggage carousel. I feel a little dazed reflecting on all of this—like it isn't real—as I stare out of the window far beyond the shoddy barricade and the vertiginous drop below, far beyond a tiny farming village in the distance and out towards where the Mediterranean Sea meets a perfect pastel sky to form the horizon.

I follow the length of that line while we move slowly over the dirt-track road and feel my worries melt away.

The heat is suffocating. The coach's air conditioning system is broken. My T-shirt sticks to my back. I wipe some sweat from my brow using the flat of my hand and then fan myself using a tattered old copy of Cosmopolitan I found folded in the mesh basket fixed to the back of the seat in front.

A worn-out dance compilation CD plays on the driver's stereo, skipping intermittently. Everyone on board is pissed. An out-of-tune singalong and shrieks in time with a chorus dissolve into cheers as the coach goes over another pothole.

The air is so thick and dry that I can taste it on my tongue. I suppress the urge to be sick, push the vomit back down my throat.

But none of this bothers me. Honestly.

Jordan's words from the airport bar play in my head in

time with the music.

A week away from reality. It's literally all I can think about. A week away from reality.

The thought turns over and over while I look out of the coach window, my gaze fixed on the horizon.

—

Hi, Mum... What? What tone of voice?... No, I'm not in a mood, it's just not the best of times for you to call, that's all... No, Mum... Mum... Mum... Will you calm down, for God's sake? Nothing bad has happened; it's just that we're getting ready to go out for the night... Yeah, I know I was supposed to have called at the airport to let you know I got here okay but it was all so hectic going through passport control and picking up the cases, and the coach was waiting outside to take us to the hotel as well, so I didn't get the chance to call and— ... Well, what do you want me to say, Mum? It's the truth. I'm sorry if you were worried, Mum, but there was nothing I could have done about it...

No, I know you don't mean to moan, and I know it's been tough for you since— ... Look, I know you want me to have a good time— ... I know you just want what's best for me... But, yeah, everything's great here— ... Yeah, of course it's hot here—maybe a little too hot, if I'm honest—but it's no big deal, I'm sure I'll get used to it...

Yeah, the place looks great on first impressions. Obviously we'll be seeing more of it in a little while... The hotel? Yeah, it's cool. I mean, it's not exactly a Hilton penthouse suite, but... Mum... Mum... Mum, you need to calm down and stop worrying. There is nothing wrong with the hotel. Yeah, sure it's nothing fancy but it's clean, so that's the main thing, right?...

So everyone back home is okay?... Great... Great... Listen, Mum, could you do me a favour and thank Aunty Kat for the holiday money she put in the bank for me? I forgot to ring her yesterday about it... And is Uncle Peter still okay to help me move my things into my digs for when I start uni?... Yeah, that's brilliant. I'm really grateful... Yeah, I know I'll

have to bring him something back to say thank you. A bottle from the duty free on the way home or something like that...
Yeah, of course I was going to ask about Grandad. I haven't forgotten about him... Mum, I went to see him the other day.... Yeah, he was okay. You know how he is these days and— ... What? Oh no, that's a shame... You'll tell him I love him, won't you, Mum?
Look, Mum, I don't mean to be rude but I'm really going to have to go because we're off out soon and— ... What's that?... Yeah, thanks for calling, Mum.... Yeah, it's been great speaking to you, too... Yeah, like I was saying, so far, so good... I've got a really good feeling about this holiday, Mum. I'm sure it's going to be a blast... So, yeah, Mum, I'll give you a call soon to let you know how I'm getting on... Love you too, Mum... Bye.
I hang up. I stuff the phone back in my jeans pocket. I puff out my cheeks and study my reflection in the bathroom mirror.
Far too pale. I should have booked a few sunbed sessions before I left. Maybe even started putting on some fake tan. I'm paranoid that I don't fit in here. Everyone we've so far encountered has a deep, rich tan and looks ripped. Everyone's a lot taller than I am, too.
I run a hand over my pasty cheeks. I wonder if I'll even tan at all during this week. I've never had much luck on that front whenever I've been on family holidays in the past, even if the last one was a long time ago.
I check what I'm wearing. A tight-fitting black Fred Perry polo. Tapered Carhartt jeans. Navy New Balance trainers.
It's weird. I know I look okay, but I just don't feel it. Something doesn't feel right.
I shake my head. I have to stop thinking like this. Not let all of the usual fears and worries affect me the way they always do.
Not now. Not on this holiday.
I just have to hold on to the thought that nothing matters out here. A week away from reality, as Jordan said in the

airport bar.
    I have to start going with the flow. Stop thinking so much. Stop living inside my own head.
    From this point on.
    I force an awkward smile in the mirror. I splash on some Tommy Hilfiger aftershave. I squirt some gel into my palm and run it through my hair.
    I shrug at the outcome.
    Strains of the guys' conversation outside filter into the bathroom. Half-expressed sentiments are punctured by half-drunk howls of laughter. "Be Someone" by CamelPhat and Jake Bugg plays through the speakers that Ewan packed.
    I try again. I give another smile and promise myself that everything is going to be okay. That it's going to be a good night.
    I wrap a hand around the stiff bathroom door handle and pull at it a couple of times before the door finally creaks open.
    The chatter ends as I step back into the room.
    We're gathered in mine and Ewan's hotel room for pre-drinks. Ewan and Jordan are each on a bed. Caleb is perched on a steel foldaway chair pulled out from under a filthy plastic table positioned against the peeling textured wall. Each taps their iPhone and stares intently at the screen.
    "Fucking hell, mate, did you have a shit? It fucking stinks in here," Jordan snorts, the white glow from his phone coating his face. "We were even wondering if you'd fallen down the bog."
    I scan the room. The walls are a sickening beige colour with dried paint chips littering the skirting boards. The floor tiles are chipped and dirty. There's a lingering stench similar to stale milk that we've tried to mask with Lynx deodorant, but it's somehow managed to make the smell worse.
    The bathroom is worse still. Pubes everywhere. All over the tiles. In the sink. Stuck to the shower floor. Different-coloured strands on the bar of soap in the porcelain dish attached to the wall.

The Heat of the Summer

But I know I have to make the best of it. That's what Ewan said when we opened the door to the room and put our luggage to one side and sat down on the lumpy, uncomfortable beds.

The silence in the room grows uneasy. Aside from the playlist, the only discernible noise comes from the Strip around half a mile from the hotel. Faint dance beats from the numerous clubs mesh into a single, tuneless drone. Wild howls. Frenzied screams. Car horns. The occasional rev of a moped.

I try to lighten the mood. "Did somebody die in here or something, lads?"

No response. Nobody looks up from their phone.

I slink over to the plastic table and grab a can of Red Stripe from the supermarket carrier bag filled with booze. I crack the ring-pull and take a lengthy slurp. The opening bars of "Miami 2 Ibiza" by Swedish House Mafia sound through the speakers.

"We've got a present out there for you, Luke," Ewan says absently.

"Out there on the balcony," Caleb adds, tipping his head towards the open balcony doors.

I walk out onto the balcony, taking sips from the lukewarm can in my hand. It's a lot cooler out here now, the temperature having dropped in the last few hours.

Neon light emanates from the Strip several streets away. A garish array of bars and clubs and fast food restaurants snaking all the way out to the sea. A steady human stream moves slowly in its direction.

I glance at the patio table in front of me to see a white T-shirt spread out in expectation of being worn. The words "VIRGIN ON TOUR" are printed across the chest in thick black capital letters. I casually pick it up and head back inside the hotel room with a carefully-crafted indifference.

"What's this, boys?"

Silence.

Everyone taps at their phones.

I clear my throat. "What's this, lads?" I ask a second time.

Jordan tosses his phone onto the mattress. He shifts upright, steadies himself and then ambles over to the table to grab another can from the carrier bag. He turns to face me. "You like it, mate?" he smiles.

"What… is it?"

Ewan pipes up. "A present. Like we said."

"We all chipped in for it," Caleb adds. "That's how much you mean to us, mate."

"Would it have killed you to fact check, boys?" I smirk. "Or are we embracing all of that post-truth shit now?"

Jordan gulps his beer. "Maybe it'll be immaterial after tonight. Here's hoping, anyway."

My face burns red. "But I'm not a virgin."

Jordan bears down over me, his prop-forward frame casting a long shadow. "There's no need to kid us out here, bud," he soothes. "We're all mates out here together. What happens on tour stays on tour, and all that kind of stuff."

"Like your cherry, hopefully," Caleb chimes.

Ewan offers a smile. "It's just a bit of fun, Luke. Don't take it to heart."

"Yeah, there's no need to have a fucking panic attack over it," Jordan remarks, grinning wide.

"But I'm not a virgin."

Jordan rolls his eyes. "Are you going to keep up with this bullshit, Luke, or are you going to wear the fucking thing?"

"It's just a bit of fun, Luke. Just banter," Caleb adds.

"Yeah, just banter," Ewan repeats.

Jordan wraps an arm around my shoulder.

"It's pretty simple, kid," he starts. "You either wear it voluntarily or we force you into it. We don't want you being a fucking stick in the mud on this holiday, mate. Because—no offence—you can be a real boring bastard at times."

I splutter something in response. I don't know what exactly.

"Luke, don't be so nervous all the time," Jordan shushes, now stroking my face. "We're only telling you this because we're your friends. We just want what's best for you. We want you to have a good time out here."

"I'm up for a good time, boys, of course I am, but..."

The half-expressed sentence echoes in the gap between songs. "October" by Icarus starts.

"Sounds to me like you've made your choice, Luke," Jordan beams.

Jordan strikes my face to leave me stunned. He then dips his shoulder to deliver a thunderous tackle to my midriff. I crash backwards onto the empty bed, the mattress compressing under our combined weight, and Jordan plants one of his giant palms against my face, pins my head to the solid wooden headboard.

A dry choke escapes my throat, heaving at the impact.

There's a sharp tug at the hem of my polo. The sound of cotton ripping at the seams. The shirt is pulled over my head and tossed to the floor.

Frantic noises leave my mouth. Wails. Cries. Pleas to Jordan to leave me alone.

"Get this on film, boys. It's got viral potential. We could end up fucking famous," Jordan laughs as he strikes my exposed torso with the back of his hand. "Let's fucking TikTok it."

I let out a yelp that sends the boys into hysterics.

Caleb gets up from the other bed, holds out his phone and begins recording.

Jordan then flips me onto my front and slips his hands inside my jeans and pulls them down to reveal my bare arse. He spanks me several times in quick succession. I reply each time with a simpering cry.

Caleb and Ewan respond to this with deep, guttural laughs that immediately shame me and, in this very instant, I wish that the earth would swallow me whole and expunge all trace of my existence.

My vision obscured by the combination of headrest and pillowcase, it's strange that I'm able to sight every bit of this humiliation in my mind's eye. I see—as well as feel—

Jordan's hands clamp around my waist, listen to him demand that I squeal as he thrusts his pelvis against my arse in pretend rape, the force of which sends the headboard repeatedly crashing against the wall.

The pitch of Jordan's voice goes up several notches, affecting it with an Asian lilt. He sounds like the Vietnamese prostitute from Full Metal Jacket.

You like getting fucked, Mr Luke? Oh, Mr Luke, ooooohhhh, Mr Luke! You like a the fuck, Mr Luke? You my bitch, Mr Luke! You my bitch! Get a-fucked, Mr Luke! Take it like dirty whore. You dirty whore, Mr Luke! You dirty whore!

He gives my arse several hard slaps at the same time.

I bite my bottom lip hard to stop myself from screaming.

Jordan's palm strikes my backside one final time. The hardest slap of all. His voice then returns to normal. "Try not to be too shit on your first time, kid," he says. "Anything longer than five seconds will be a good result."

Caleb falls into a fit of uncontrollable laughter.

Ewan slides across to the other side of the bed and picks up the VIRGIN T-shirt from the floor. He hands it to Jordan.

"Best of luck tonight, bud," Jordan says, ruffling my hair after getting to his feet.

Caleb moves back a couple of steps and repositions the camera to get a shot of my throbbing red arse.

Jordan unfurls the T-shirt. He clasps a palm across my forehead and peels me back from the headboard. I cry out as the T-shirt is forced over my head by all three of my friends.

Quiet descends on the room.

I'm in the foetal position.

I roll over to see Jordan leaning against the plastic table clutching a beer, flanked by Caleb and Ewan, both staring at their phones again.

Jordan takes a gulp of his beer without removing his gaze from me. "You'll thank us for this, Luke," he says. "Trust me, you'll thank us soon enough."

3

"Jesus, Luke, are you going to be like this the whole time we're out here?" Jordan asks, glancing over his shoulder at me a few steps behind the group.
We're on our way to the Strip.
I scratch my neck. The T-shirt irritates my skin. I cross my arms over my chest to cover the "VIRGIN ON TOUR" message. I keep tugging at the thing in the hope that it will extricate itself from my body.
There are smirks and giggles and pointed fingers from passers-by aimed in my direction.
We move through a human swell. In between tanned and tight bodies. In between people wearing fancy-dress costumes. In between groups clad in matching printed T-shirts. In between people not wearing much at all. People in swimwear and mankinis and dental-floss bikinis. Superheroes and cartoon characters. A group of lads around our age dressed in retro football kits. Another as old-school wrestlers. Some girls in Pink Ladies jackets.
A gang of a dozen or so girls dressed in pink T-shirts with nicknames printed across the front cuts past us. COWGIRL CARLY. DIRTY DAISY. BLOWJOB-LIPS BECKY. They spot my T-shirt and screech excitedly. They grab me and pull me alongside them. They pinch my swollen arse. Squeeze my dick hard. Make comedy sound effects.
Ewan pulls out his phone and takes a photo of me sandwiched between ANAL ANNA and SUZIE 69. I'm bright red, drenched in sweat. I shy away from the lens, wearing an expression of sheer discomfort as the girls peck my cheeks.
The Strip stretches out for a mile or so. Neon-lit bars and clubs on either side span its entire length. Dance music spills out into the street. A constant pounding as regular as a heartbeat. Rihanna's voice, in particular, seems to be everywhere. One song merges with another so it's impossible to tell if she's singing about falling in love in a hopeless

place in one direction, or about diamonds in the sky in another. There are people milling around outside each bar and club with the name of the venue printed on their T-shirts trying to entice large groups inside with offers of free shots and free fishbowls. The pulsing music drowns out their voices most of the time. Indecipherable white noise engulfing the night. Broken bottles and fast food containers and used condoms litter the street alongside shallow pools of blood and vomit.

But it doesn't appear to bother anyone. People are too busy having a good time. They're out of their minds, kissing and groping each other. Bodies are packed tight together. Hands stuffed down pants. Clamped around pert tits.

—

"Are you going to be like this the whole time we're out here?"

Jordan asks me this again while we are in a club at the far end of the Strip.

Rihanna's voice sounds distorted and distant, yet strangely close and clear at the same time. The message that this—all of this—is what you came for blares as Jordan orders a round of Sambuca shots.

It's the sight of me standing here at the bar all awkward and uncomfortable, shifting my weight from one foot to the other and repeatedly folding my arms across my chest, which compels Jordan to speak.

He glares and asks the question a second time.

I can't keep pretending not to hear him.

I'm drunk but without the happy buzz that usually accompanies the feeling. Instead I'm paranoid that every eyeball in the club is fixed on me wearing this T-shirt.

I lift my head to see Jordan's face bathed in strobe lighting.

"Are you going to be like this the whole time we're out here?"

It's the last thing I remember of the night.

The Heat of the Summer

The first thing to register is how much my head hurts. Then it's how dry my mouth is. My eyelids flicker, but I close them shut as the sunlight forcing its way into the room through the glass balcony doors strikes me square. I drag my palms across my face. I let out a deep, raspy groan and pull the thin duvet cover tighter over my chest.

It's when I roll onto my side that I become aware that there is someone next to me. The unexpected feeling of my fingertips brushing against cool skin. The sensation jolts my eyes wide open.

It takes a few seconds for me to adjust to the light. For my head to stop spinning.

The girl I'm lying beside is tanned and broad-shouldered. A little chubby with some creased folds around the base of her back. Her hair is long and black, draped over her shoulders, half-concealing a Playboy Bunny tattoo. Her share of the duvet is tangled around the lower half of her body, exposing a snippet of arse crack. The contours of her body slowly contract with each drawn-out breath and the occasional snore.

The mattress croaks as I get out of bed.

I'm naked. My dick is still semi-hard.

I look around the room to see that it's in an even worse state than the previous night. The sunlight casts a cellophane sheen over the peeling walls and chipped floor tiles. The stale-milk smell attacks my senses and I suddenly come over all queasy. I grab a half-drunk bottle of water from the bedside table and unscrew the cap and gulp as though my life depends on it.

Ewan is still asleep in the bed next to mine. He's completely naked on top of the crinkled sheets. A girl is spread across his body starfish-like. She's slender and tanned with blonde highlights in her hair. She's also naked, sound asleep. Both she and Ewan appear dead to the world. The pillows and duvet covers are all bundled together in a heap on the floor.

I finish the bottle of mineral water in a few deep

mouthfuls and find that my mouth is still dry as hell. I shuffle towards the bathroom and glance back over my shoulder, gaining confirmation that neither girl is especially pretty.

Ewan's is possibly the more attractive of the two at a push.

I force open the bathroom door. I grip the chipped sink basin with both hands, like I could fall backwards at any moment, and sight myself in the mirror.

I'm ghostly pale. Red-eyed. My hair is a complete mess. Copper-tinged stubble has sprouted from my chin.

I wash my face and then brush my teeth to strip the taste of death from my mouth. I move to the toilet and try to force a piss.

My dick hurts. A noticeable throb. There's a burning sensation when the piss eventually does come out, which prompts a pained wince.

I then head back out into the cesspit of a hotel room. I'm unsteady on my feet, still drunk. I stagger through the minefield of discarded clothes and bedding, and move over to the open suitcase propped against one of the table legs and grab the first pair of boxer shorts that I lay my hands on. A tight navy blue pair imprinted with images of SpongeBob SquarePants and Patrick Star. I slip them on, rearrange my cock and balls.

I look down at the overflowing waste paper bin beside the suitcase and see that the T-shirt I wore last night is stuffed inside, buried under some beer cans and glass Coke bottles. I pull it out and spread it across the plastic table. The "VIRGIN ON TOUR" message has been crossed out in red marker pen.

I can't help but raise a smile.

I ball up the T-shirt and toss it back into the rubbish bin and then cast my attention out of the glass balcony doors at the perfect blue sky. I slide open the doors and step outside and find that I'm unable to look at anything else.

Caleb's voice breaks my concentration. "Morning, shagger."

The Heat of the Summer

I turn my head right to the adjacent balcony to see Caleb and Jordan sitting at their patio table. They're both bare-chested and sporting sunglasses, each wearing only a pair of swimming shorts. They're playing cards. Both have a can of Red Stripe in front of them with a family-sized bag of Lay's crisps ripped open in the middle of the table.

"Finally off the mark, huh, Luke?" Jordan grins.

———

The next few days blur into one.

The same routine is followed. Swimming pool. Beach. Bars. Clubs.

It seems time moves slower out here, mirroring the feeling of lethargy engendered by the heat. The hours drift without urgency. There are aimless stretches of daytime during which it feels like there's nothing to do but watch the sky gradually darken and the neon lights of the Strip turn on.

There have been girls. Sex games. Drinking contests on the Strip.

There have been foam parties and pool parties.

Laughing gas and balloons. MDMA hits. Bumps of cheap coke.

I'm happy out here. I've found that I've finally learnt to let go. Learnt to calm down. Learnt to live in the moment. My inhibitions have definitely lowered and I've had a blast.

I've stopped overthinking. I've started to go with the flow.

———

There's one incident which sticks in my mind. A foam party held in one of the clubs. The whole thing descended into an orgy. Jordan ended up fucking a girl against the wall. Both of them were covered from head to toe in foam.

We were at the beach the next day. We were spread across sun loungers, each of us doing nothing but absently gazing out towards the horizon.

Jordan piped up that he wasn't sure if he raped the girl from the party. No-one said anything. As though the words meant nothing at all. The silence gave way to Jordan's guttural laugh. We all followed his lead before another silence elapsed to consign his words to memory.

The waves lapped the shore in front of us.

We returned our focus back out towards the horizon and thought of nothing.

—

The nights resemble a reel of TikToks.

One seeps into the other to the point where they become interchangeable. Virtually indistinguishable. Equally as disposable. One night bleeds into another without any real point, purpose or definition. Fun just for the simple hell of it.

We've all enjoyed ourselves out here. We've all had the time of our lives.

I don't think any of us want it to end.

—

Hi, Mum... No, I know I haven't called— ... I'm sorry but— ... Mum, would you let me finish, please?... No, I'm not raising my voice. I'm not getting mad... Mum, you need to calm down. Everything's fine.

Yeah, I'm having such a good time out here, Mum. This place is unbelievable. The weather's been fantastic. Just so warm and lovely. And I've got an okay tan going on as well... I know, can you believe that, Mum?... I mean, don't get me wrong, I haven't gone as dark as the rest of the boys, but it's a better tan than I thought I'd get... Yeah, Mum, this place is something really special. We've done so much and got on so well and all of my worries about stuff back home, they've just disappeared. This holiday has been exactly what I've needed... What's that? Drinking? No, we haven't drunk as much as you probably thought we would.

But, yeah, what I was saying before about all the worries from back home... Yeah, exactly, this holiday has really helped take my mind off things... You know how sometimes it helps if you take a step back from something to see it in a completely different light? Well, that's what it feels like I've done... You know how I was really anxious about starting university? About moving away to a whole new place away from my friends and family and living on my own in digs? Like, talking panic attacks and cold sweats during the night and stuff like that? Well, it doesn't seem such a big deal anymore... Don't get me wrong, I'm still a little nervous about it, but now it feels like it's something I can handle. I think I've realised that sometimes you've just got to go with the flow and take everything as it comes.

So how is everything back home?... Right... Okay... Okay... Look, Mum, I understand you're having a bad time at the minute, but there's nothing I can do about it out here. I'm literally thousands of miles away from home and... Yeah, yeah, sorry, yeah, you're right, that did sound a little bit rude. I honestly didn't mean for it to come out like that... I'm sorry to hear that about Grandad. I hope he's feeling much better soon enough. I know the pills can take it out of him... Uh-huh. Yeah... Look, Mum, you'll keep me posted, won't you?... No, don't worry, you wouldn't be making me worried on holiday.

Look, Mum, I've really got to go now. We're heading off out for dinner soon, so— ... Yeah, it's been great talking to you, too. Give my love to Grandad, won't you? Tell him I've been asking about him... Thanks. Thanks... Yeah, I promise I'll call you again soon to let you know how I'm doing. I promise I won't forget, Mum... Really, I promise... Love you too, Mum... Speak soon... Bye.

I hang up and slip the phone inside my pocket. I make my way back across to where we are sunbathing.

It's stifling today. So hot and humid that even walking a few feet is enough to sap a person's energy.

The beach is packed. Barely a square metre of free space. Rows of prostrate bodies bake on sun loungers. Zero movement from anyone. A few small groups usually play volleyball or kick a ball around, throw a Frisbee or take turns to jump into the sea, but there's nothing like that happening today. It's as if everyone has submitted to the heat. Everybody is lying lifelessly in complete silence, content simply to stare dead ahead at the sea through the tinted lenses

The Heat of the Summer

of their sunglasses.

I get back to my lounger exhausted. I collapse beside the boys and catch my breath and wipe the sweat from my brow.

The conversation immediately cuts out, as it always tends to whenever I return to the group.

But I've learnt not to let this bother me so much. I'm not really thinking about it at all, in fact. I'm content to just go with the flow. Take whatever as it comes along.

The quiet lasts for a few minutes. All of us stare open-mouthed at the horizon. The heat keeps us pinned to the sun loungers.

Jordan tips his head to the side, clears his throat. "Was that your mummy on the phone, Lukey?" he asks in a mock baby voice.

His sunglasses make his expression inscrutable.

"What? Oh, that? No. No, it wasn't," I respond.

"Then who was it?"

"Nobody."

"Nobody?"

"Well, nobody important, at least."

The answer appears to satisfy Jordan. He resumes staring straight ahead and reaches blind for the beer resting beside him.

I allow the silence to settle, take in the soft roll of the waves and the intermittent squawking of birds before angling my head in Ewan's direction.

"Hey, mate," I begin.

Ewan directs his attention at me.

"You know those girls we fucked on our first night out here?"

"Yeah?"

"Can you remember their names?"

Ewan pauses, looks through me. "Does it matter?"

His reaction prompts me to cast my eyes back out to the sea. "I guess not."

The sun beats down. The sky is a resplendent blue. A shade that I assumed only existed in a child's imagination.

Jordan decides to get a tattoo. Tally marks on the underside of his left wrist. He wants five. Because that's how many girls he claims he's fucked out here. But he adds that he wants to make sure there's enough space for new additions.

He then says we should all get tattoos to commemorate the holiday. Says we should all get similar tally marks. We all agree, and throw our arms around each other in the middle of the dancefloor with "Nothing Really Matters" by Tiesto bouncing off the walls.

—

But we all soon change our minds while detouring off the Strip to a dimly-lit tattoo parlour. Except for Jordan, that is. He's the only one still determined to go through with it.

He's pissed. We all are. But he's a different kind of drunk to us. On a totally different wavelength. Surly. Aggressive. Mean. He takes our refusal to go through with his idea as a personal affront.

He stands imposing in the doorway of the ramshackle parlour. Scowls.

"Fucking pussies," he spits, splintering the wooden door frame with a sequence of furious punches. His knuckles cut open. "No fucking fun," he slurs in between shots. "No fucking fun at all. Fucking arseholes. Fucking limp dick cunts. I'm fucking sick of you all. Every fucking one of you. Fucking fannies."

We try to calm him. But none of us make much sense. Our words are sloppy and stilted, drowned out by the tides of dance music from the nearby clubs.

It all passes through Jordan.

He takes particular issue with my attempts at placating him.

He sits down on the kerb and cradles his head in his hands while muttering obscenities. I sit down beside him and extend an arm across his shoulders, only to have it batted away. I try a second time. But the reaction is the same. This time he does it with so much force that I fall backwards onto some broken glass littering the pavement.

I'm too drunk to feel anything. Too drunk to even think properly.

I get to my feet. "Don't ruin the night like you always fucking do," I shoot back. "We're all friends here. Or fucking supposed to be."

—

I don't want to go home. I like it here. I like the person I've become.

I've only ever been unhappy at home.

I wouldn't say I've had a bad life as such. I've never been mistreated. I've always been supported.

But at the same time it's like I've never been able to escape the sadness which has hung over me for as far back as I can recall. I can't honestly say for certain whether I was simply born like this, or if it's because so many sad things have happened to me that it feels like they have measured out my life.

And that sense of sadness has only grown the more I've dwelt on these kinds of thoughts.

I've always resented myself for being this way. Partly it's because I feel I have no right to.

I know I've largely had it good. I know there are countless others who have had a far worse time of things in life.

But, still, I can't help the way I feel.

But I'm free of all of that out here. Unburdened. I didn't feel this way at first, admittedly, but it's something that's crept over me.

It's hard to pinpoint exactly when I found myself letting go. Maybe it was while idling away a whole day at the beach. One of the nights when I got blackout drunk. Getting high for the first time. Maybe it was even losing my virginity, even though I can't remember much about it. I guess they've all had an effect in helping me forget everything.

But then when I think about having to return home at some point and leave every bit of this behind, I find the sadness returns in insurmountable waves. So I try my hardest to push it away.

And then I feel happy again.

4

I was eight when Ruby came along.

I can remember my parents telling me the news. They sat me down in the living room one Saturday morning and said I was going to be a big brother. The reason I can vividly remember it happened on a Saturday was because my parents made me mute the cartoons for a moment. That made me think it was something serious.

I remember feeling a little guilty at first because my mood didn't immediately correspond with that of my parents. How elated they were. I smiled and hugged them both and asked questions in an excited voice about whether the baby would be a boy or a girl. When it would be born. How long it had been growing in Mum's tummy for.

But I was uneasy about the whole thing. About how much things would change. Whether my parents would still love me as much. It occurred to me even then that their attention would surely be divided between me and the new baby.

My parents spoke to me about gaining responsibility. They talked about the importance of setting a good example and being a good big brother. But I wasn't sure what they meant. Would I have to change? Didn't my parents like the person I was? Wasn't I enough for them? What if the baby didn't like me?

My head filled with all of these confused thoughts and all I found I could do was smile and pretend that I was happy at hearing the news. Because it was what my parents wanted to see.

———

Ruby was born on a Tuesday. My parents were singing that song when I met her for the first time. I thought they had made it up on the spot, or had at least been working on it while at the hospital. It was of course years later that I found out if it was a Rolling Stones song. I had always meant to ask my parents whether they actually named her after the song or whether it was a coincidence, but neither really spoke much about Ruby after she passed away.

I stayed with Grandad while Ruby was being delivered. I always loved sleeping at my grandparents' house as a kid so an extended stay was a real treat. Ice cream after dinner every night. Free reign of the television. A later bedtime. I know it sounds ridiculous, but I had somehow managed to forget the reason why I was even staying there until Grandad passed the phone to me so Dad could provide an update and check how I was doing.

I'm not sure if I even took in what he said, looking back. I think I just wanted to get off the phone as quickly as I could and get back to playing video games.

—

My parents kept it a secret from me that they were out of the hospital. The knock at my grandparents' door came while I was playing FIFA. I paid it no attention until I heard Grandad cooing out in the hallway. I hit pause and stepped out of the living room. Grandad moved to one side to offer me a glimpse of my baby sister wrapped in a pink shawl being cradled in my mother's arms. My father started singing "Ruby Tuesday" and tickled her chin. Mum smiled and joined in and gently rocked Ruby from side to side in time with the song.

Dad noticed me staring. He beckoned me closer and then squatted on his haunches. He draped his giant arm over my shoulders and asked if I wanted to meet Ruby.

Mum leaned forward and opened her arms slightly so that I could get a better look at my little sister.

I scanned her perfectly round face and full rosy cheeks. Her button nose. The wisps of black hair matted to her milky, flaking scalp. Her eyes were shut but fluttering delicately as though dreaming.

I remember I smiled.

5

We're back at the beach. It's as if we haven't left.

The same spot. The same debilitating heat. The same clear sky and bright blue sea stretching out for miles.

Jordan shifts on his lounger. He's finding it hard to get comfortable. He lifts his arm from behind his head and scratches at the tattoo on the underside of his left wrist. The area appears inflamed. A violent shade of red. He sighs contented at the temporary relief offered by fingernails against raw skin.

The waves roll. Birds squawk.

The only noises breaking the silence.

It makes the feeling of Jordan directing his stare at me all the more pronounced.

I pretend to ignore him. Hope that it will make him forget what's on his mind. I keep staring at the sea.

"You enjoying yourself, Lukey Boy?" Jordan asks.

I haven't heard him.

Just like back at the airport bar. Just like on every night out we've had since being here.

Jordan repeats the question. "You enjoying yourself, kid?"

His voice is sterner this time.

I tip my head towards Jordan and give a lazy nod. A tepid smile.

"You sure?" he responds.

"What do you mean?"

Jordan rolls onto his front, sights me over the rim of his Aviators. "You've been a fucking disappointment all holiday, you know that?"

An awkward laugh leaves my throat.

"No, I'm fucking serious," Jordan insists. "I'm fucking sick of you. You're a fucking bore, man."

I shake my head. "What do you mean? Is this about the other night at that tattoo place?"

"It all adds up, kid. All contributes to the feeling I have," he says. "It's like you're always judging us. Always there silently in the background like a fucking ghost. We get that you're shy, but it feels like something bigger than that now. As if you think you're better than us or you're somehow above this place. You don't talk. You don't suggest anything fun. If you had your way, we'd probably just spend all our time in the hotel room pulling our dicks and playing cards."

"Jordan, I honestly don't know what you're talking about, mate. What the hell has brought this on?"

I look to the sun loungers either side of me. First at Caleb. Then at Ewan.

They both pretend this isn't going on. Both stare dead at the sea.

Jordan removes his Aviators to give me a hard stare. "I'm going to level with you here, Luke," he starts before motioning at Caleb and Ewan with the stem of his sunglasses. "Both of these dickweeds here vouched for you. They had to convince me to allow you to come on this holiday. It was just going to be three of us because I told them I could see you being nothing but hard work. I was certain you wouldn't enjoy it. That you'd spend the whole week inside your head. Just like you do at home."

He stops for breath, checked by the heat, and continues. "But Caleb and Ewan felt sorry for you. They thought it would be unfair to leave you at home with your crank mother while we were out here having the time of our lives. They said that being out here would be good for you. That it would somehow open you up. But do you know what, Luke? I've been proven right, haven't I?"

Jordan glances at Caleb and Ewan.

"Isn't that right, boys? You two were wrong. And I was fucking right."

Caleb and Ewan release the same zombie grunt. Both still staring out to sea.

"Mate, I honestly don't know what you mean," I choke. "I've never once thought I'm better than anyone here or that this place is beneath me. I've had an absolute blast out here. I've had the time of my life."

Jordan shakes his head. His sunburn glows. "You're not listening to what I'm saying. And that's the problem. You never fucking listen, Luke. You're lost in your own little world inside your head."

"What are you trying to say?"

"That I'm fucking sick of you, Luke. I'm sick of everything about you. How boring you are. Your stupid mannerisms. That air of superiority you give off. I've always been able to just about put up with it at home because we've never been in the same space twenty-four-seven, but it's been hard managing you out here. I can't deal with you anymore. It's such a fucking struggle."

I remain silent, looking blankly at Jordan.

There's nothing more I can do. Nothing more I can say.

It takes all of my strength not to cry.

Jordan lies flat on his sun lounger. He puts his Aviators back on. He locks his fingers together and positions his hands behind his head in a relaxed pose. His position mirrors that of Caleb and Ewan, both of whom are still motionless. He joins them looking out at the sea.

—

Around twenty minutes of terse silence provokes me into making an excuse to leave their company. I can't recall what I say the second it escapes my mouth. Something about needing to stretch my legs or needing a drink. I don't suppose it matters, really.

I put on my T-shirt and prise myself off the sun lounger.

The boys let me walk away. In peace. Alone.

—

Maybe Jordan was right in a weird way. He was brutal, no question, but maybe his general assessment of things was correct. Maybe I am far too inhibited. Too shy for my own good. And maybe, in turn, it has fucked up my ability to form anything approaching a normal relationship with anyone. I've had the exact same set of friends since I was a little kid. Now, I'm at the stage where it feels like none of us have anything in common.

The Heat of the Summer

And I was the last of those friends to lose my virginity. And of course I'm the only one of those friends to have never had a girlfriend. And I'm the only one of the group who has had to call their mother every day at some point.

Maybe it's all connected. Maybe my issues are so deep-rooted and so intertwined that knowing what I need to do to get my head together is an impossible task.

Maybe all of this is part of the problem with me. That I spend too much time thinking. Analysing and worrying. Deliberating and agonising. Constantly tossing back and forth between different things.

I know it. My family know it. The boys know it.

I was sure that I'd changed out here. That I had stopped taking every little thing to heart. That I had stopped overthinking. I was certain I had finally managed to cut loose and go with the flow.

But clearly I was wrong.

It must have all been in my head. Something that I'd convinced myself was true.

So now I'm wondering where I go from here. Should I try a little harder to become somebody that I'm not? Should I embrace things a little more? Show the boys that I actually am having fun? Show them that I've changed as a person? Or at least pretend that I have a little more convincingly?

My phone vibrates in my pocket.

I let it ring out for a minute or so.

I don't even bother checking to see who it is.

6

I must have walked for around a mile and a half since leaving the boys. I look up to find that the scenery around me has changed without my even realising.

This part of the beach is a lot quieter. Sparsely filled. I've left behind the zigzagging rows of toasted bodies spread-eagled across plastic sun loungers. I turn around for a moment and sight far into the distance where the beach curves around like a fish hook to see them all as insignificant specks in the distance.

It's mostly locals around me. An elderly couple hold hands while walking barefoot as the sea laps the sand. Parents play with their young children. Some kids who look about two or three years younger than me are involved in a game of beach volleyball.

I feel out of place here. So awkward and skinny and pale compared to everyone else around me.

A cool breeze tickles the back of my neck. Laughter from the volleyball game drifts within earshot.

I meander in the direction of a beach bar built into an embankment leading up to the island's old town. A snapshot of whitewashed facades and stone archways and narrow cobbled streets.

Strains of Diplo's remix of "Old Town Road" fill the air. I approach the beach bar, see that it's Hawaiian-themed. A mural is splashed across the outside wall featuring a surfer dude catching a big wave as shark fins poke from the water around him. Tiki torches protrude from mounds of sand outside the front entrance, either side of rows of steel tables. A few have been pushed together by a large group of twenty-somethings completely engrossed in a card game while drinking cocktails.

I may as well grab a drink. Kill some time.

Try to forget about what has happened.

The air conditioning blasts me stepping inside the bar. The mechanical whir of the system undercuts the song.

The Heat of the Summer

Cheap Hawaiian paraphernalia in abundance. Polynesian statues spread out across the floor. Masks fixed to the wall behind the bar. Pictures of grass-skirted hula girls and framed stills from an old-looking cop show. Hawaii Five-O, I guess.
All pretty garish. But I guess it will do.
At least it's quiet.
There's a chubby girl alone at the bar. Two guys playing pool. A young couple sipping cocktails sat at a table on a raised platform.
I sit down on a stool at the bar. I order a Heineken.
The barman plucks a bottle from the cooler and sets it down on a white paper napkin. I bow my head, feel myself zone out. I start tearing at the edges of the paper napkin and then at the beer bottle label.
"You okay?" a soft female voice to my left asks.
I turn my head towards the chubby girl, a bar stool separating us. Her smile emits warmth, instantly attracts my attention.
She's actually quite cute. Olive-skinned with hazel-coloured hair tied back in a ponytail. She's dressed in a billowing turquoise T-shirt and a pair of ripped denim shorts.
"Sorry?"
"You okay?" she repeats in a light Welsh accent. "The way you're shredding that bottle label, you're giving the impression you haven't been laid in ages."
A nervous laugh leaves my throat.
"Because you must be the only person on this island not getting any, in that case," she follows up.
I nod, roll the torn pieces of paper into cigar shapes. I sigh and glance down at the tiled floor.
A few seconds' silence.
"Seriously, is everything okay?" she sings, angling her body to face me square, appearing concerned. "You look fed up."
I nod again, sup my beer. Give a pained smile. "Just a rough day," I say eventually.
I turn my head and look around the bar. The Polynesian

The Heat of the Summer

masks. The framed TV stills. Try to look anywhere but at the face staring straight at me.

"Do you mind if I sit here?" she asks, gesturing at the empty stool.

"Go for it," I shrug, watching the barman stack the dishwasher.

She sits down next to me.

"Want to talk about it? Is there anything I can help with?"

I shake my head and then cast my eyes around the bar.

"I'm not sure you'd want to hear me out. I'd probably just end up boring you or something."

"Babe, don't be ridiculous. I'd be happy to talk if there's anything you want to get off your chest. I've been here on my own for most of the day anyway. Trying and failing to get that barman's attention. Real shame. I don't think he's into Welsh girls much," she grins.

"How come you're here on your own? Where are your friends? Or your boyfriend?"

"No boyfriend, trust me, babe," the girl giggles. "My friends have gone off to some water park outside of town. It didn't take my fancy, to be honest. Not really my scene."

"How come?"

She lifts her T-shirt up over stomach to show a pale potbelly made all the more striking in contrast with her tanned complexion. The girl smirks and playfully slaps her stomach before rolling down her T-shirt.

"That's why."

"What?"

"My fucking gut, babe. I'm made to feel like a whale out here. Everybody is shredded. It's like they've all been airbrushed or something. I've never been the most secure person in my own skin anyway, to be honest, and I find this place can really do some damage to your self-esteem if you're anything less than perfect. So I could do without a day of feeling self-conscious at a water park, to be honest with you."

"I think you look fine."

The Heat of the Summer

"Thanks," she smiles. "But you're a terrible liar."
Silence.
The air conditioning system hums. The quiet clack of one pool ball striking another in the background.
"What's your name anyway?" the girl asks me.
"Luke."
"I'm Emma," she says.

The bar has started to fill up at this point. There's a tactile young couple in their early thirties several bar stools down from us. A small group of locals sat at a table around seven feet away chatting loudly to one another. The twenty-somethings from outside now crammed in a booth, continuing their card game.

The barman sets a fresh round of drinks in front of us.

"Right, Luke," Emma begins, taking a sip of her cocktail. "I don't know how you've managed this, but you've so far managed to escape telling me why you came in here looking so glum. Like a real fucking sad sack. There may as well have been a black cloud hanging over you."

"Just one of my friends," I reply. "He's been a bit of a dick these last couple of days."

"How come?"

I shrug. "I don't know. He accused me of being boring. He said I'm no fun. That I've given the impression that I find this place beneath me or something."

"So what do you think gave him that impression?"

"Because I'm a quiet person, I suppose," I say. "I can be quite shy at times."

"There's nothing wrong with that."

"That's what everybody tells me. Especially my mum."

"Do you feel like it's a problem?"

I let out a sigh after a long sip of beer. "I don't know. Maybe. Sometimes. See, I just wish I could cut loose sometimes, you know? Forget everything and live in the moment. But I often can't, no matter how hard I try. I seem to absorb everything like a sponge. Every little bad feeling.

The Heat of the Summer

Every bad thing that happens. I wish I could forget about stuff and let it go. But I just can't seem to. Everything ends up turning over and over inside my head to the point where it feels as though I'm torturing myself."

Emma puffs her cheeks. "There's a lot to unpack there, Luke."

I nod. "I know. The funny thing is that it felt like I had become a different person out here. I could literally feel all of my anxieties leave me. It felt like I had put real distance between myself and my worries back home."

"What sort of things worry you back home, then?"

"Just the usual stuff, really," I reply. "Family. School. You know."

I take another mouthful of beer to stop myself talking.

Emma leans in closer. "Look, some things can't be helped worrying about. It's natural. It's not ideal, but it's just life. The key is to just take things in your stride. See them for the little things they are. To be honest, it sounds to me like that's exactly what you've done out here. If you feel like you've left your worries behind, then who cares what some dickhead thinks? He doesn't know what's going on inside your head, does he?"

"I suppose."

"And this guy doesn't seem like much of a friend to me anyway. He sounds like a prick. So what if you're shy and quiet? It's nothing to do with him, is it?"

"Jordan's okay. Most of the time. He can just be a bit intense. It's just who he is. He gets off on pushing people's buttons."

"I think you could do without people like him in your life, Luke. I don't mean to sound twee, but you have to embody the kind of change you want. You even said that you've found yourself relaxing out here. That's all that matters. You have to be true to yourself. And that's something I've learned the hard way, you see. You can't be someone you're not in an attempt at appeasing somebody you'll never be able to make happy."

"Yeah, I know what you mean. The thing is we've all been friends since before we can remember. Since reception class. And it's hard to just let go of that kind of history, isn't it? Even if you've become different people over the years and drifted apart without ever really acknowledging it. Like, how do you just break things off and get new friends?"

Emma smiles. Her face lights up. "Look, Luke, you're a good person. You shouldn't be so hard on yourself. I know that change can seem scary and I'm not going to lie, it often can be. But you have to believe it will be worth it. And that comes from personal experience. It's sad to say, but happiness often doesn't come easily. But the first step is accepting yourself for who you are and freeing yourself of any negative influences."

I nod in response. "Yeah. I suppose."

"There's no suppose about it. I know what I'm talking about. Trust me. I've been there."

"So what's your story, then?"

Emma slurps the dregs of her cocktail. "Get out your wallet and buy another round, Luke. This could take a while."

—

We get to know a little bit about each other over a few more drinks.

She tells me she's twenty. Two years into an English degree. I mention that I will be starting a degree in Film Studies in September.

And then I tell her about all the anxieties that come with that. Moving away from my family. My friends.

But she tells me not to worry. That it will all be okay.

I've heard people say things like this to me a hundred times before. But the understanding look that greets my broken speech, her full brown eyes taking everything in, the way she places her hand on top of mine and grips tight in response to hearing my fears—for the first time in a long time, I truly believe somebody when they tell me this.

I tell Emma about my family. I tell her how my parents

are no longer married and haven't been for some time. I tell her that I have few happy memories of them together. That the long silences and the poorly-concealed fights dominate my thinking whenever my mind drifts back. Muffled noises through walls late at night. Abrupt shushes whenever one sensed I was nearby. The front door practically flying off its hinges after a cross word. They're the sort of things I end up thinking about.

I tell her about Grandad. I tell her that he hasn't been well for a while. How he has good days and bad days, and how there seem to have been a lot more of the latter recently.

But I don't tell her about Ruby. That would be too much.

Emma wells up through all of this. I'm not sure if it's the booze, but she seems genuinely taken aback. By my honesty. By my admission that all of this stuff has made me the mess I suspect I'll always be.

Emma then tells me about herself.

"You're not the only person around here who feels they're fucked up. Like they're completely neurotic," she responds through clenched teeth, her eyes all moist and red.

She tells me about being bullied at school on account of her weight. How she came to self-harm as a teenager. She tells me how she would lock herself in the bathroom and castigate herself for being ugly and fat, hurl insults at herself until she was hoarse. Until the blood flowed to her face. She describes how she would then take a razor blade and cut her wrists and her legs from joint to joint while hyperventilating.

She says it always made her feel better. It instilled a feeling that she was in control. That she was finally doing something about her issues.

But the relief that came was only temporary. She tells me how that initial rush of positivity would inevitably elapse into a darker, more aggressive depression. Signal a period of despising everything about herself. The way she looked. The way she spoke. Her emotions. Her whole thought process.

Suicide crossed her mind on occasion. But something would always bring her back, thankfully. Quiet moments of clarity during which she realised the depression didn't define her.

She often thought of her grandmother during such spells. How when she was a child she would often fall asleep listening to her tell stories.

Or she would take her dog on long walks along the beach close to where she lives. When there would be no-one else around and she could walk for miles without encountering another soul.

She shows me the only scar that's been unable to fully heal. A faded but still noticeable vertical line around four inches in length on the underside of her left wrist.

Emma says that she found the courage to tell her parents what she had been doing. She went to therapy. Started taking medication. She began to settle and learnt to shut out the negativity. She got to know herself a lot better. What calmed her. What made her happy. The things she didn't need in her life.

"I still have hang-ups. But I feel as though I'm getting better at dealing with them. It's a long process, Luke."

—

The bar succumbs to an early-evening lull. We decide on a change of scenery. We go for a walk along the beach.

"Better or worse than the beach back home?" I ask Emma.

"Different," she replies. "A lot different."

We walk slowly. Talk quietly.

The conversation lightens. We speak about our likes and dislikes. Films. TV. Music. The usual things.

The temperature cools. The tide rolls in.

We kiss further along the beach. Miles from where we met.

—

We journey into the old town for the night, moving in the opposite direction to the crowd heading towards the flashing lights and pounding music in the distance.

We meander down winding cobbled streets which diverge

from each other to lead nowhere in particular. It's a whole other world perfectly confined to a few square miles.
    Quaint bars. Charming restaurants. A picturesque town square fenced by flowers in full bloom and ivy-wrapped stone relics.
    A string band plays up-tempo music. Locals drink and dance happily, sing along to traditional folk songs.
    We watch this unfold, completely entranced. We grab a table outside one of the whitewashed bars lining the square and order drinks and some seafood to share. Lemon-soaked calamari. Garlic-buttered prawns. Mussels in a white wine sauce. Whitebait with mayonnaise. We split a loaf of freshly-baked bread to mop up the leftover sauces and share a bottle of white wine as the square fills around us.
    We sit and talk and let the hours fall away.

―

We eventually call it a night. I'm not sure at what time exactly. We're both drunk and exhausted at this point.
    She invites me back to the apartment on the edge of the old town where she is staying with her friends.

―

Morning comes.
    We're out of the door before Emma's friends wake up. We head back into the old town for breakfast. Coffee and pastries from some bakery on the corner of one of the old town's splitting streets that I don't think I'd be able to grasp even if I lived here.
    The image of the place, its intricate layout, vanishes from my mind practically the second we step outside and walk back to the apartment.

―

Time spirals from us the very same way it did yesterday. The afternoon comes around in an instant.
    Emma gets emotional. She and her friends fly home tomorrow. She wipes away a couple of tears and tells me how great it was to meet me. How she wished we could have met a lot sooner.

The Heat of the Summer

I wrap my arms around her and pull her in close. I even find myself getting tearful. I tell her that we'll keep in touch. That we'll visit each other regularly. That we'll give it our all to make this work.

Emma nods and nuzzles her head into my shoulder. My T-shirt soaks up her tears.

She leaves so she can start to get ready for a night out with her friends. She mentions that she would like me to meet them. They're all going to some club called Pandemonium down at the far end of the Strip, she says.

I tell her I'll be there. That I'll definitely see her later. That we'll have a great final night together before picking things up back home.

The Heat of the Summer

7

Hi, Mum... What? No, nothing's the matter, Mum. Calm down, please, for God's sake... Well, you've been moaning that I haven't called, so I thought I would, to let you know how things are g— ... Yeah, yeah, everything's been great. It's been an amazing experience. It's been a blast from the minute we landed. It's going to be a real shame to leave because this holiday's been everything I expected and so much more. We've only got a couple of days left but I wish we could stay a lot longer. I don't mean that to sound like I'm not missing you and everyone else back home and of course I'm looking forward to starting university, but you know— This trip has been just what I've needed. It's really put me in a really positive state of mind.

And I've met a girl, Mum. She's great. Her name is Emma and she's twenty and she's going into her last year of university in September. You'll love her, Mum. She's really intelligent and she's funny and she has such a great personality. She really is amazing, Mum. We've spent a lot of time together and we've been getting really close these past couple of days. I think there's a real connection there. We're definitely going to stay in touch and— ... What? Jesus, Mum, how about we both get home and settle back into things before we make arrangements about meeting family and stuff like that, huh? ... No, Mum, I know you don't mean to be like that. I know you're happy for me.

But I've never felt like this before about anybody, Mum. I don't want to be getting too deep into things but, at the same time, I'm really excited. This holiday has really helped me with a lot of my anxieties. The future doesn't seem as scary to me now.

Look, Mum, it's been great talking to you about this. I'm really looking forward to seeing you and the rest of the family again soon. I'll give you a call in the next day or two, sometime before we leave ... Thanks, Mum ... Yeah, I love you too. Give my love to everyone back home and I'll see you all really soon ... Yeah ... Yeah ... Love you too, Mum ... Bye.

We moved to a new house a year or so after Ruby was born. Dad got a promotion at work. It meant he was a lot busier and often stayed late at the office and usually came home way past my bedtime.

The house was much bigger than our old one. It had a huge garden, which I immediately fell in love with. I remember asking Mum and Dad if I could have goalposts set up so I could play football and they promised that they would buy a set for me as soon as they had finished unpacking.

The garden seemed enormous to a nine year old. I remember counting my steps from one end to the other only to forget halfway. I likened it to Wembley in my head, because I suppose that was the largest patch of grass I could conceive. The garden sloped at the far end and led down towards a small kidney-shaped pond. Tall trees sagged over the fence from the house opposite to cover it in perpetual shadow. Dad took me down there the day we moved in and I remember seeing a couple of tadpoles swimming around and a frog on the opposite side squat motionlessly as though staring us out.

I remember Dad telling me that I would have a lot of fun down this part of the garden. That I could make nature pictures out of the multi-coloured leaves that fell from the branches of the low-hanging trees, or do research projects on the frogs and the tadpoles that lived there. He said that he would even help me build a den, and because of how far it was from the house it would be like a secret hiding place. But then he either corrected himself or forgot what he had said and told me that I was to only go down to the pond if either he or Mum were in the garden. I told Dad that I was a good swimmer. But I don't think he heard me.

I remember going around each empty room on the day we moved in and claiming them for different uses. Ice-cream parlour. Video-game room. Mad-scientist laboratory. My parents humoured me and played along, but they were keen to remind me that I was no longer an only child. Mum, in particular, laughed and asked where Ruby would sleep. I shrugged my shoulders because I hadn't considered her.

It was a detached house in a peaceful tree-lined street that I remember thinking looked like something straight from the cookie-cutter Nickelodeon shows I was hooked on as a child. The neighbourhood was idyllic. Nice and quiet. It showed how much money Dad was making at the time, which of course I had no concept of. All I could think about as we drove along our new street was that there was a real chance I would find it all a little boring because I couldn't see any evidence of kids around my age living nearby.

Mum and Dad worked hard getting the house up to scratch. My grandparents chipped in whenever they could. It seemed as though there was a constant stream of handymen at the door during the first few months we lived there.

The house was practically a husk the day we moved in. Empty rooms. Exposed floors. Bare walls. I remember comparing the desolation to a house's skeleton in my head. I was looking at its bare bones. It was an image I struggled to shake even when the house was fully decorated and we had lived in it for a while.

I remember hearing strange noises the first few nights in that house. It must have been my imagination because nobody else heard anything.

I really struggled to sleep. I heard a jangling sound whenever I tried to close my eyes. My head would hit the pillow and I wouldn't be able to stop myself from speculating what was happening outside my door. I heard floorboards creak. Pipes moan. I was sure of the slow creep of footsteps stopping outside, the light visible through the gap under the door obscured at certain moments. Sudden bangs in the dead of night.

My parents told me not to worry whenever I brought up the issue. I was told old houses made a lot of noises. It was just what they did.

The Heat of the Summer

I started wetting the bed again. I had allowed myself to think I was over it after being dry for the previous two or three years. Instead it came back worse than ever. A recurring nightmare. That I wasn't far away from secondary school only compounded my worries because it was obviously the sort of thing that big kids didn't do.

My parents weren't overly concerned, which was a surprise because I assumed that they would be angry. They put it down to the stresses of moving. The feeling of being in a new bed and adjusting to new surroundings. I guess I knew they were right deep down, but it did little to ease my fears. It made me feel as though this was simply something I would have to put up with for the time being.

But all I kept thinking about was how this thing I was so ashamed of had come back after I thought I'd beaten it. The new house had brought it back.

One thing which excited me was the promise of a games room on the third floor. Opposite another room Dad had said was going to be his study. He said that he would get a pool table and a dartboard and a foosball table in there and we could play a lot of games together and I said that I wouldn't want to leave the room until I became better than him at each one, but he laughed and said that would probably take a while.

The study was completed pretty quickly. But he never got around to starting the games room.

One of the rooms on the ground floor was to be a nursery for Ruby. That was Mum and Dad's first port of call. They dumped the baby holdall stuffed with food and formula in there and Mum kept Ruby occupied while Dad set to work assembling the flat-pack cot.

That was on the day we moved in. It gave me the chance to explore the skeleton house on my own.

Not that there was much to see, but I remember thinking that each of the rooms seemed vast without any furniture or decorative features. My voice echoed, sounded incredibly loud and commanding, which was something I had never

The Heat of the Summer

experienced indoors before. The ceilings were so high, and I can recall wondering how Dad would get up there to paint them. He would at least need a much taller ladder than the one we kept in the garage at our old house.

I moved apprehensively from room to room. I was fearful that I would see something I wasn't expecting. I think it was a general worry stoked by the absence of any feelings I usually associated with a house. Comfort. Warmth. Security. In my mind it made it all the more likely that I would encounter a dead body in the middle of one room or a loitering ghost or even a murderer lurking on the other side of a closed door.

I eventually made my way downstairs. I pushed open one of the doors to see the shell of a living room. There was a bi-folding glass door at the far end of the room which offered a glimpse of a conservatory on the other side. Light streamed in from outside to cast a sickly yellow sheen across the beige walls.

The key was inside the lock of the glass door. I turned the handle and stepped into the conservatory. It was the only room in the house that had proper flooring. Black and white check tiles similar to a chess board. It wasn't an especially hot day outside, but I can remember how the heat struck me as I made my way across the floor, the glass-panelled walls intensifying the sunlight. I walked to the opposite end, where the light was at its brightest. I pressed my hands against the glass and squinted hard as my eyes slowly adjusted to my surroundings.

I think that was when I saw the garden for the first time.

—

I tread along the hotel hallway towards the room Ewan and I share. The ceiling lights flicker. The stale-milk smell invades my nostrils. A sickness forms in the pit of my stomach.

Drunken laughter spills out from the room and rackets around the hallway. The noise meshes with "Cola" by CamelPhat, seeping through the door all distorted and tinny.

The choke of my key turning in the lock chimes with the

The Heat of the Summer

howls from inside the room. The door creaks. I step inside at the exact moment before the beat drops and my friends are instantly silenced, each locking their eyes on me.

"The wanderer returns," Jordan exclaims, lifting a can of Budweiser to his lips.

"So, what have you been up to, then?" Ewan follows.

I shrug my shoulders. "Nothing much. Exploring."

Jordan grins. "Exploring the inside of that pig we saw you with this morning, you mean?"

"What?"

"That pig we saw you with this morning," he repeats. "We decided on a little wander around the old town earlier to mix things up and saw you going into some coffee shop or café or whatever with this fat girl. It looked like you were both into each other. Very touchy-feely. You both reeked of sex. We could smell it on the pair of you from the other side of the street."

"Don't... don't talk about her like that, mate," I respond. "She's not a pig—"

"Well, she fucking looked like one, Luke," Jordan roars. He lifts up his white V-neck T and slaps a palm across his swollen red belly before clamping an inch of fat. "I know I've put on a little timber this holiday, man, but she was ridiculous. My fucking God. Has she spent her entire holiday in McDonald's?" He slurps from the can and presses his nose with the middle finger on his opposite hand to make a crude pig snout. "Oink, oink."

Ewan and Caleb cry laughing.

"Don't call her a pig," I say.

"It's just banter, Luke. Lighten up. We're just messing with you. Don't take everything so seriously," Ewan cuts in.

Caleb dips into a supermarket carrier bag, pulls out a beer and forces it in my hand. He then taps my cheek. "Chill, mate. Just have a beer and forget about it."

I crack the ring-pull, flick some foam from the rim and take a swallow.

"We don't mean anything personal, mate. It's all just fun

and games," Ewan adds.

Jordan nods. "Yeah, exactly. If you like getting stuck into fatties, that's your business, kid. It's all just fun and games down on the farmyard."

Jordan thrusts his pelvis, gulping from the can. The action prompts more laughter from Ewan and Caleb. Jordan then puts down his drink and swings his body towards Caleb and clamps his tree-trunk arms around his waist. Caleb laughs and swears in the same breath and tries unsuccessfully to break Jordan's hold. Jordan manoeuvres his giant palm around Caleb's neck and forces him down onto my bed, bending him over, pinning his face to the pillow.

Caleb flails and cries for Jordan to stop.

Jordan slides Caleb's jeans down over his backside. He slaps the bare, peachy arse with the flat of his palm. The noise of a cracked whip.

Caleb yelps.

Jordan then pretends to fuck him from behind. "Oink, oink, oink, oink, oink," he snaffles after each thrust.

Ewan laughs, starts filming with his iPhone.

I watch on motionless.

This goes on for a little while longer. Jordan peels himself off Caleb and then gives his pulsing red arse one last hard slap. He picks up his beer can from the floor. He takes a step towards me, extending his hand.

"Come on, Luke, we're just fucking with you. Don't take things to heart. Things are said and quickly forgotten about. What happens on tour and all that kind of stuff, kid."

I say nothing. My eyes flit between Jordan's face and his outstretched hand.

I then glance over at Caleb, who is shuffling upright with the aid of the headboard. His lips are firmly clenched. An ashen look spread across his face.

"Come on, Luke. Don't be a dick about this," Jordan insists.

I shake his hand.

"Good to see you're not taking this badly, Lukey Boy. So

what's the girl's name, then?" he asks after a mouthful of beer.

"Emma," I mumble.

"What?"

"Emma," I repeat louder.

"And you and Emma... are you planning on seeing any more of each other before the end of the holiday?"

Jordan poses this question while forcing his finger inside a hole made by pinching his thumb and index finger together on the opposite hand.

I shrug. "I was going to see her and her friends tonight, actually. They leave tomorrow. That's why I came back. To change."

"Where are you all going?" Ewan chips in.

"Pandemonium. Down the far end of the Strip."

Jordan necks the last of his can. "You wouldn't mind if we tagged along, would you, kid? It is our holiday as well, after all. Plus, we haven't seen much of you these last few days, have we, Lukey? I'm interested to see if you've grown some bollocks since our little chat yesterday." He pauses to reach down and clamp his hand around my balls. "You've certainly emptied them, haven't you? You fucking dirty dog."

The noise of Ewan replaying the video of Caleb's pretend rape cuts the silence.

"Anyway, back to Miss Piggy," Jordan continues.

"Don't call her that."

"Yeah, right, Emma, sorry," he replies, rolling his eyes. "Anyway, do you think any of her friends would fancy hooking up for a final fling?"

I shrug again.

Jordan beams. "I think we'll tag along anyway. It is a free country, after all. And I wouldn't mind getting a kick out of watching Luke pull out his best moves on this fat bird."

He paces over to the carrier bag on the table and grabs a can from inside and tosses it over to me. He pulls out another can. Cracks it open. Gulps it back. Belches.

"Plus," he continues, "if Emma's friends are even half the

size of her, I'm sure we could all go for a good old-fashioned game of poke the pig, eh, lads? What do you reckon? Twenty notes each in the pot?"

Jordan's eyes flit between Ewan and Caleb. He wipes a trickle of beer from his chin.

8

"One last roll in the pigpen for you tonight then, Luke?"

Jordan says this to me as we shuffle side-by-side towards the far end of the Strip, trapped in human traffic. Ewan and Caleb are several steps behind, heads bowed, lost in their phones.

Music blares loudly from the clubs on either side of the street. Screams and shouts and mangled snippets of conversation from passers-by rattle our ears. Elbows prod my ribs. The late-evening air is thick and muggy, enough to make Jordan's questions all the more tiring.

We trek towards Pandemonium. Weave between packs of bodies. Pace past spaced-out weirdos out alone. Blank the club workers trying to get us into their bars with the promise of free drinks. Free shots. Free fishbowls. Free whatever else.

I notice a kid a few yards to my right slumped against a kerb, surrounded by burger wrappers and broken bottles and empty nos canisters. Thick globs of vomit stain his polo shirt. The whites of his eyes are glazed. A couple of people pause to take selfies.

I look left to the balcony jutting from a club. A tanned blonde girl dressed in a white summer dress and a pair of high white stilettos sets down her glass and trots inside the club along with her friends as "Physical" by Dua Lipa starts up. Somebody drops something into her drink practically the second she turns her back.

We pass a fast food restaurant. Kansas Fried Chicken. I glance through the window. A small, slight kid takes a punch to the temple from a much bigger guy, who looks at least five years older. The guy unloads a series of swift stomps to the kid's chest. The kid curls into a ball like a hedgehog. The fast food workers behind the counter yell at the older guy to stop, but the attack goes on. The kid coughs up blood. The clientele sat at plastic tables watch this happen, craning their necks towards the attack while skewering chips with plastic forks.

"So you'll be going back to the pigpen tonight, then?"

This is what Jordan says to me as we make our way to the tail end of the Strip.

An imposing structure comes into focus. A grey exterior several storeys high with tinted windows. Crimson searchlights on top of the structure probe the night sky. Dance beats travel in our direction, thicker, heavier with every step to the point where it feels as though music is playing inside my head. A glowing red neon-lit archway curves over the entrance to spell the name of the club.

PANDEMONIUM.

"What a fucking woman. Jesus."

I catch Jordan saying this during a split-second break between songs.

We're at the entrance to the club. I turn my head to see him pointing at a promotions girl standing to the right of the cast-iron curved entrance, busy handing some slips of paper plucked from her bum-bag to a large group of boys.

She looks to be in her early twenties. Tanned. Tall. Long catwalk-model legs. Her body is perfectly toned. A head of dirty-blonde hair flows down over her shoulders. She's dressed in a tight-fitting black tank-top with "PANDEMONIUM" written across her chest in red letters, along with a pair of black denim hot pants.

She's stunning. All I can do is nod in agreement with Jordan.

My phone vibrates. I take it out from my pocket to see a text from Emma asking for my ETA. Another message comes through saying she and her friends are already inside close to the bar. A love heart emoji instantly follows the second message.

I fire off a reply telling her we're outside. That I'm looking forward to seeing her again. I hit send but find that the message bounces back after a few seconds. I tap resend a couple more times but still have no luck.

We file towards the entrance.

The promotions girl dressed in the black tank-top and hot

pants approaches us.

"Free shot, guys?" she chirps, handing us each a paper voucher imprinted with the offer.

"Wow," I blurt.

The boys snigger.

The girl appears bemused. "Well, that's an enthusiastic response."

"What's your name?"

The question leaves my mouth without thinking. I tense. That sinking feeling.

The girl smirks and stares straight through me. "Crystal."

"I'm Luke."

Jordan's booming laugh in my ear.

"Have a nice night, boys," Crystal says, stepping past to interact with the group behind us in line.

The entrance gapes. We step under the threshold and file down a steel-panelled tunnel leading us into the belly of the club. The decline is deceptively sharp, causing my calves to ache as I try to get my balance. I press my palms flat against the metal wall to steady myself, feel the coldness against my skin. The low, sloping ceiling is inches from the top of my head.

"Panic Room" pulsates through the tunnel. Soundwaves ripple my skin. The darkness in front of me is dense and impenetrable. I keep moving forward, deeper into the black, towards the noise. Short blasts of hot breath moisten the back of my neck.

The music intensifies. I snatch for air.

The metal floor levels under my feet. The music pounds at a deafening volume, as I move closer to its source. It becomes apparent that the tunnel is widening as my hands can no longer trace the steel panels.

Flashes of blinding white light burst through the pitch black to illuminate the inside of a heaving club.

A human wave rises and crashes in time with the music.

The tunnel funnels us into a human swell. Heads bob, arms flail around us. Sweat drips from the low ceiling. A sea of glazed expressions is revealed in unexpected bursts of light.

I hear Jordan's voice.

"Spotted the whale yet?"

The action is confined to one shoe-box room in this massive building. An underground bunker.

Everyone is packed in tight. Body to body. Tension throbs. A thin layer of steam hangs above our heads.

The tangible anticipation of a chorus drop.

"No," I find myself murmuring.

I scan the club, crane my neck around the marble pillars evenly spaced across the dance pit. I cast my eyes further, over to the DJ booth on top of a podium at the far end of the club, where a ripped bald black guy with a beard, wearing sunglasses and a white tank-top, holds sway over the crowd. He raises a left fist high into the air and pumps it in time with the beat, orchestrating the pit of manic limbs below.

Everyone is on top of each other. The DJ arches forward and extends an open hand to the pit.

Bodies surge forward. A raucous scream goes up.

I look over to the L-shaped bar to the right of the DJ booth, towards the row of people perched on bar stools, where I finally see Emma and her friends.

Jordan's voice sounds.

"Where's the whale?"

"I'm not sure," I lie.

He presses his lips to my ear.

"I'm not sure you'll be able to perform tonight, anyway. I think you shot your load talking to that girl outside."

"What?"

"The promotions girl," he says. "All she did was hand us some vouchers for free shots and you acted like it was an invitation to get into her pants. You know, you can be so fucking embarrassing at times, kid."

"Look, leave me alone, okay?"

His laugh synchs with the music.

"I'm honestly not joking when I say this, but it's like

The Heat of the Summer

you've got a disability or something, mate. It's like you're incapable of playing it cool with any girl even remotely good looking. It's probably why you were able to talk to that fucking whale so easily."

I'm about to turn around and bite back, only for Ewan to interrupt.

"Where is your girl, anyway, Luke?"

I give a cursory look around the club, angling my neck in different directions before settling on the bar.

"Over there," I say, pointing.

We struggle through the crowd in single file.

"So," Jordan begins, "do you have protection with you?"

"A condom?"

"No, a fucking harpoon," he roars.

Flecks of his saliva strike my cheek.

We reach Emma and her friends at the bar, and I immediately feel self-conscious.

Emma is delighted to see me, beaming as her eyes lock on mine. She shuffles off the stool to grab me in a bear hug, planting a hard kiss on the lips.

Jordan pushes his nose into a crude snout out of the corner of my eye. His mouth makes the shape of some pig noises which are lost to the music.

Emma introduces her friends to mine. No-one hears anybody's name.

It's an awkward encounter. Conversations are largely unheard. The snippets that are audible come over all stilted. The two groups eventually pair up and go elsewhere out of obligation.

Jordan places his hand against the small of the back of the girl he's taken as he walks away.

I'm distracted. I catch myself constantly looking away at the DJ getting everybody pumped up. At the other couples making out under strobe lighting. At some promotions girls emerging from the tunnel and merging from the crowd. Looking everywhere and anywhere but at Emma.

Emma, meanwhile, is all over me. She brushes my arms

The Heat of the Summer

and my hands. She plays with my hair and then wraps an arm around my waist and pulls me in close.

I look away. Look around the club again.

I'm trying to play it cool. Trying not to make a big deal of things.

Emma talks incessantly. Her lips flap soundlessly against the relentless tide of the music. I fake interest in whatever the hell it is she's saying. I nod and shake my head in all the right places, give monosyllabic responses whenever her mouth relaxes.

I think I'm seeing her in a different light tonight. I'm starting to believe that what happened between us may have been one of those "in the heat of the moment" things. A perfect occurrence of vulnerability and circumstance. Nothing more. Nothing less.

I zero in on some blonde promotions girl standing by the entrance. I'm certain it's Crystal. I watch her talk to a small group of people dressed in the same Pandemonium attire, and then keep my attention fixed as the group disperses around the club and merges with the revellers in the pit. She flits around the place, moving between different groups, engaging in small talk. Our eyes meet briefly from a distance of several feet and she immediately glances away and takes a couple of euro banknotes from the guy she's been talking to. She stuffs the money inside her bum-bag and I track her as she skirts the outer edges of the club before disappearing up the tunnel leading out onto the Strip.

A heavy-set guy in a motorcycle helmet and a black leather jacket carrying a gym bag passes her on the way. He hands the bag over to a young kid collecting glasses, who then heads down an exposed passageway behind the bar. The motorcyclist turns his back and exits the club.

"Are you okay?" Emma asks me.

"What? Oh, yeah. Fine."

"You just seem a bit distant tonight," she says. "Are you sure you're ok—"

"Emma, babe," I interrupt, "I'm really sorry, but would

you excuse me for two seconds? I feel a little bit dizzy. It's really hot in here. I think I just need some fresh air."

She attempts a response but the jarring noise of static and feedback plugs the split-second silence. We instinctively turn our heads towards the booth on the podium high above the pit, where the DJ is perched unsteadily on top of his sound system clutching a microphone.

The pit erupts.

The DJ draws the microphone to him and looks out across the swell. He licks his lips. Grins.

"WELL, IT'S ANOTHER GOOD FUCKING NIGHT OUT HERE IN FUCKING PARADISE. AND IT'S ANOTHER GOOD FUCKING GOOD NIGHT HERE IN THE BEST FUCKING CLUB ON THIS WHOLE FUCKING ISLAND... PAN-DE-FUCKING-MONIUM. YOU KNOW THE FUCKING NAME."

Frenzied cheers.

A tear rolls down the cheek of the guy directly in front of me.

The DJ's deep booming voice shakes the club.

"THIS NIGHT IS JUST GETTING STARTED."

Screams. Cheers. Whoops.

Arms in the air.

"AND I'M GONNA BE THE ONE TO TAKE YOU SOMEPLACE ELSE."

Screams. Cheers. Whoops.

Arms in the air.

"AND YOU KNOW MY FUCKING NAME. K... O... MOTHERFUCKING... S. LET ME HEAR YOU ALL SAY MY FUCKING NAME."

A cry goes up which dissolves into a fierce one-note chant.

K-OS! K-OS! K-OS! K-OS!

"YEAH, YOU ALL FUCKING KNOW IT. NOW LET'S GET BACK TO THIS SHIT. BECAUSE THE PARTY DON'T STOP OUT HERE. IT... NEVER... FUCKING... ENDS!"

The Heat of the Summer

A huge roar shakes the ceiling. Paint chips shower the pit. The chant slows and then settles into a steady rhythm.

The DJ soaks it up. Sticks out his chest. He stretches his arms wide above the pit and bears an immaculate bleached smile. He pushes his sunglasses further up the ridge of his nose and puffs his cheeks. He pauses for several seconds, waits for the pit to tire itself out

There are gasps. Hands are pushed back over people's heads, fingers rushed through hair. Foreheads are dabbed with the backs of palms. Faces set in the same wide-eyed astonishment.

Intermittent squeals. Yelps. Excited howls.

K-OS! K-OS! K-OS! K-OS!

The DJ presses the microphone to his lips again.

"AND I WANT TO SEE YOU ALL AT THE FUCKING BOAT PARTY TOMORROW. NO FUCKING EXCUSES. IF YOU AIN'T THERE, YOU BETTER BE FUCKING DEAD. I WANT YOU ALL TO GRAB THE NEAREST HONEY YOU SEE WEARING PANDEMONIUM GEAR AND GET SOME FUCKING TICKETS. I SEE YOU ALL TONIGHT. I SEE YOU RIGHT HERE. I'M TAKING PICTURES. I'M MAKING FUCKING NOTES. AND I EXPECT TO SEE EVERY FUCKING ONE OF YOU AT SEA TOMORROW TO CARRY THIS ON. WE DON'T FUCKING STOP OUT HERE. WE NEVER STOP. THE PARTY GOES ON FOREVER OUT HERE. EVERY FUCKING DAY. EVERY FUCKING NIGHT. NON-FUCKING-STOP."

The pit breaks into a collective scream. The whites of eyes shimmer in the darkness.

A mic drop. Strobe lighting. K-OS hits another song.

Bounce. Bounce. Bounce.

I excuse myself to Emma and venture back up the tunnel.

The fresh air strikes me cold.

Early hours of the morning. The Strip is in full swing.

Intersecting hordes. Indecipherable cries. Pumping music. Blinking neon.

The Heat of the Summer

Crystal is close by. She goes along the queue to my right distributing vouchers.

I step towards her.

"Hi, Crystal."

She slides some euro banknotes into her bum-bag, turns to face me. "Oh. Hi," she replies vacantly.

"Can I get some tickets for the boat party tomorrow? The one that the DJ was talking about?"

"Oh. Yeah. Sure. How many do you need?"

"Four."

"Eighty euros."

I reach inside my wallet and hand her four twenty-euro notes to practically clean me out for the remainder of the holiday. She folds the notes inside her bum-bag and hands me four small tickets which look as though they've been made on a home PC.

Crystal turns her back and is about to resume working her way down the line, until I clear my throat.

"So how long have you worked out here for?"

She stops. Turns back around. Sights right through me.

"The years all kind of roll into one at a point. It's hard to say exactly," she shrugs.

An awkward silence. All the more pronounced against the backdrop of white noise.

"Yeah, I know what you mean," I eventually say. "I've only been here around a week and it feels a lot longer."

She turns her back a second time.

"So is it fun working here?" I ask.

She waves at someone walking along the Strip and then glances back at me over her shoulder.

"Sorry, what?"

"Working here," I repeat. "Is it fun?"

"Pays the bills, I guess."

She turns her back again.

"Is the money good?"

She shoots back at me, her face displaying annoyance. "Look, you seem a nice kid and everything, but I'm busy

The Heat of the Summer

here. This isn't a holiday for me, you know. I have to work."

She nonchalantly flicks back her hair and puts on a kind and courteous smile, approaching a group of four lads in the queue.

I'm left motionless. Stunned by the outburst.

"Oh, sorry," I mumble into the elapsed dead air.

She works the line. Goes through the motions.

An alluring smile. A flick of her dirty-blonde hair. A flirtatious comment.

9

I'm back inside the club now, back deep in the bowels of Pandemonium, where it feels suffocating. My chest is tight and fat beads of sweat are dripping down my face, and I'm struggling through the crowd, jostling for room in an effort to get back to the bar.

Heavy sound waves emanating from the giant speakers wash over the pit, flood the senses.

I force a path and wade through with my arms out in front of me until I'm eventually able to see everyone again.

They're all at the bar. My friends are sidled close to Emma's.

Emma, meanwhile, is still sat on the same stool in the exact same spot as before.

I tap Jordan's shoulder. He turns around and lowers his phone, the screen's glow lighting his face.

"Guess what I've done?" I start.

He stares at me disinterested.

I pull the four boat party tickets out from my pocket and wave them under his nose.

"Only gone and bought us four tickets for that boat party tomorrow at twenty euros a pop, haven't I?"

A wide grin immediately forms on Jordan's face. He presses his lips first to Ewan's ear and then Caleb's and whispers the news while jabbing his finger in my direction. They both mirror his expression as he breaks from them, the realisation settling.

"That's what I'm fucking talking about," Jordan yells over the music, first giving my back a hard slap and then wrapping me in an almighty hug. "The boy's only gone and got himself back in the game, hasn't he?"

Ewan and Caleb clamber on top of me in celebration. My knees buckle and I end up in a heap on the congested floor.

But I'm too busy laughing, too busy enjoying the acclaim of my friends to care.

My eyes flit between Emma and her friends as I'm pulled

The Heat of the Summer

to my feet. They each give the same bored, unimpressed look.

Caleb cries out for shots. The girls are forgotten about and a couple of shots of Sambuca are lined up along the bar and quickly thrown back.

I hit black-out drunk soon enough. The praise of my friends and "Bullet in the Gun" the last things I hear.

—

I come around like I've been shaken and slapped around the face. I tune back into my surroundings, the neon lights of the Strip at first hazy and distant before starkly coming into focus.

The warm air makes me feel nauseous. The humidity clings to my skin.

I struggle forward and spew up a little over my shoes, but manage to force the rest of the bile back down my throat.

I glance around to see that I'm the only one of the group out here. I pull out my phone and send texts, only to have each one bounce back at me as people exiting the club jostle past, elbowing and nudging me off balance.

Crystal is visible through a gap in the zigzagging bodies. She's standing alone on the kerb outside the club. She takes drags of a cigarette with her arms crossed as though bored, occasionally looking left and right down the long, winding street.

I stumble through the crowd to get close.

"Crystal... Crystal... Crystal," I call over.

My voice is drowned out by the music spilling from the neighbouring clubs. Surrounding cries. The revs of mopeds and scooters.

She still has her back to me as a silver convertible pulls up alongside her. The guy behind the wheel is around forty-ish and has a resplendent tan and cropped salt-and-pepper hair. He's wearing sunglasses and a pristine white buttoned-down shirt that practically glistens against his skin. He looks relaxed with his arm draped out of the window. Not a wrinkle, not a blemish on him, as though his skin has been ironed free of creases. He glances at Crystal and motions at her impassively.

She circles the car and hovers around the door of the passenger seat. They briefly exchange words. Both appear to show no emotion. She eventually gets inside and straps herself in and, as I struggle through the bottleneck, the driver hits the accelerator and the car shoots off along the Strip and out of sight, the engine's snarl fading from earshot.

I remain still for a few minutes, gazing open-mouthed in the direction in which the convertible disappeared.

More people have exited the club at this point, an amorphous throng enveloping me.

I look over my shoulder to see the lads emerge from the tunnel. They're each paired with a friend of Emma's. They blend into the surrounding crowd and I watch as they shuffle towards the beach before slipping out of sight.

I turn back to see Emma making her way out of the tunnel with her arms folded over her chest. Her face is bright red and sweat-soaked. Thick strands of her hair stuck to her forehead. Dark circles prominent under her eyes.

I head over, pushing through the crowd moving in the opposite direction. She tips her head to the ground and walks at a steady pace in the midst of the swell.

I sidle up to her and fold an arm across her shoulders.

"Hi, babe," I slur.

Emma flinches. She bats away my arm.

"You've got some fucking nerve, you know," she spits.

"Woah, babe—"

"And don't you fucking dare babe me after how you've acted tonight."

"What are you talking about? Calm down. Tell me what the matter is."

Her eyes widen. "And don't you fucking dare tell me to calm down, either. You really don't have a fucking clue, do you?"

"Look, I don't get this—why are you so angry all of a sudden?"

"I'll tell you why I'm so angry, Luke. I'll tell you why, right now," she seethes while pushing me away.

We're both stationary at the kerb outside the club. The dead-headed throng bends its movement around Emma and me. The argument fails to elicit so much as a flicker of a response from the crowd.

"You've made an absolute show of me tonight, Luke," Emma continues, her anger turning to upset. "You've made me feel like a fool."

"What? But I don't get this—"

She shakes her head. "You've made me feel worthless, Luke. As though the time we spent together meant nothing to you. I've done nothing all day but tell my friends what a great guy you were. How you were different to any other boy I'd met. And then you turn up with those clowns you call your mates and you put on this stupid, immature front. Those same mates that you spent so much time criticising yesterday. The very same group of mates you had no qualms saying had made you feel so bad about yourself."

"What are you getting at here, Emma?"

"It's my last night here, Luke. I thought we could have spent it together. I figured you'd meet my friends and then we could go off and do our own thing again like we did yesterday. Maybe talk a little bit more about what we're going to do when we're both home. You know—firm up our plans."

"Well, things just happen, don't they?" I snap. "Not everything happens the way you expect. Life doesn't always work like that."

"What's that supposed to mean?"

"If my friends want to tag along, there's not much I can do about it."

"But you don't have to lower yourself to their level, do you? You don't have to put on some act and be somebody you're not. It's as if you've been embarrassed to be seen with me tonight. You've been rude to me. You've practically ignored me. Whenever I've tried to talk to you, you've brushed me off with grunts and one-word answers. And you haven't been able to take your eyes off the fucking sluts who work at this place. I've been sat literally inches from you and your friends and I've heard every word you've said to each other. Are you really this insensitive, Luke? You've hurt me tonight, you know. Really hurt me."

"I can't be bothered having this discussion with you. You're pissed. You don't know what you're talking about."

"What? And you're stone-cold sober?" she snorts. "There's sick on your fucking shoe. You look like shit."

"Oh, give me a fucking break. I'm on holiday. Things just happen, don't they? Not everything has to mean something. Not everything has to go according to a plan, does it? Happily ever after and all that bollocks. We spent one night together, Emma. One fucking night. It's not a great deal in the grand scheme of things, is it?"

Emma looks stunned. It takes a few moments for her to respond.

"Well," she gulps, "that's pretty obvious now."

"Look, we had a good time together, but... Let's not make it out to be something that it wasn't."

Tears stream down her cheeks. "I thought I knew you, Luke. I thought you were different to most people. But I guess I was wrong, huh?"

I shrug my shoulders, put on a brave face. I ignore my pounding headache and the knot in my stomach.

"Well, I can't help you there, Emma," I say. "Sorry about that."

Her eyes are bloodshot. She covers her face with her hands and slumps to the ground to sit cross-legged right in the middle of the passing crowd, still shifting around us in one steady unbroken motion. Emma's shoulders start to tremble. She lets out an anguished howl.

I can't bear to look at her at this point.

I turn my back and stumble into the middle of the human swathe and slide in the opposite direction to where my friends and Emma are headed. There's a ringing in my ears that's compounded by the music assaulting me from every angle.

—

I'm back in the hotel room. Alone.

I don't know where Ewan is. Presumably with his girl. Neither Jordan nor Caleb is in the room next door.

I don't know what time it is.

I'm tired. But I can't sleep.

The room is a mess. Clothes are strewn everywhere and rubbish has spilled over from the waste paper bin and there are empty deodorant cans and aftershave bottles lying horizontally all across the floor. Nos canisters. Coke residue. Our beds have been unmade since the first morning here. Tangled duvet covers. Exploded pillowcases. There's still the faint smell of sick, that we've been unable to conceal.

I've taken some painkillers.

I bought some beers from an all-night supermarket near the hotel and I'm currently nursing one while sitting at the plastic patio table. I'm tilting back in my chair with my bare feet crossed on the table top. I reach for one of the empty cans and crush it in my palm and then take aim at the mound of rubbish protruding from the waste paper bin, only for it to land around six inches from my target.

There's nothing going on inside my head right now. I'm not thinking of anything at all. Simply killing time.

I get up from the chair, my back suddenly stiff. The harsh scratch of the legs scraping over the tiled wall echoes. I wince as I straighten up and stagger over to the balcony doors. I slide them open and step outside.

I pace to the edge and look out at the glowing neon pocket in the middle distance, reminding me of a scene from Blade Runner.

Aimless snippets of noise drift through the air. Screams. Threats. Laughter.

Strains of the music undercut everything. A constant background noise.

I draw the can to my lips and take a mouthful and then

dangle my arms over the side. I take a long look down at the people passing by below, who are unaware that I'm watching them.

—

I wasn't a good brother to Ruby. That's not to say I didn't love her. Of course I did. I loved her a lot. More than I ever thought would be possible when my parents told me the news that they were having a baby.

But I can't say I was a good brother after what happened.

I found being an older brother strange at first. Especially after being an only child for so long.

I mean, most people with younger siblings tend not to know any different. Normally the difference between a first born and a second born is four or five years tops. Your memory isn't fully formed at that age. It's difficult to remember things with any great certainty. I imagine for people like that it must feel as though their sibling has essentially been a part of their life from as far back as they can remember.

But that wasn't the case for me. You already have a fair idea of what's going on at eight years old. You can remember things. You can hold a conversation. Your personality is beginning to form.

Things have a habit of sticking out at that age, too. Real minor stuff you're still able to recall God knows how many years later. Like how I can still remember Dad telling me that the police would arrest me and send me to kids' jail when I refused to put my seat belt on properly when I must have been five or six. Or how fearful I was of "the man" who would snatch me away if I didn't hold my mother's hand tight enough.

The point I'm making is that at the age I was when Ruby was born, you're already filled with all kinds of worries and concerns that ultimately shape you as a person.

And I think that's why I found it difficult coping with Ruby's arrival. Because my personality and memory were already developed to an extent. I can distinctly remember a time before Ruby was born and a time after she was born. I can recall the effect her arrival had on my life. How much my life had changed, from being an only child who was the sole focus of my parents' attention to suddenly being seen as a responsible older brother. Mum and Dad spoke to me about setting a good example and all of that stuff, but they were tough concepts to grasp when I had spent my life up to that point doing whatever I wanted.

It was a culture shock, to say the least. One I didn't handle well at all.

Kids aren't great at comprehending conflicting emotions. I don't think any of us are, in fact. It's why I think I struggled to process how I could possibly feel two completely different emotions towards Ruby. And I think it skewed my impression of her as a result.

Which I know sounds ridiculous because she was only a baby.

I couldn't work out how it was possible to love somebody so much, but also be struck by such all-consuming jealousy.

I definitely loved her. I know I did. That feeling is still there inside me. She melted my heart the very first time I saw her. The first time I ever made her laugh when I blew a raspberry in her face is still fresh in my mind, because I don't think I had ever heard a sound as pure and innocent. Complete, unbridled happiness. I loved playing games and watching TV with her and being allowed to hold her in my arms when Mum and Dad were nearby. Things like that have stayed with me all this time.

But I was jealous of her at the same time. No doubt. I resented how she occupied most of my parents' attention. How it felt like I was of secondary importance to them. How it seemed like they didn't love me as much as they did before Ruby came along. It sounds stupid because Ruby was not in control of her actions. She had no way of knowing how I felt. It wasn't her fault. It wasn't even the fault of my parents. They were taking care of her the same way any loving parents would.

I accept it was all down to me. The different ways in which I lashed out, trying to make sense of my emotions. It was nobody's fault but mine that I got into fights and started messing about at school, giving teachers a hard time. It was all down to me that I was horrible to my parents and did stupid stuff out of spite – like flushing my dad's car keys down the toilet after watching Bart Simpson do it on an old Simpsons episode. I even started hitting my mum whenever she was busy with Ruby or was tending to household chores. Basically any time I felt I wasn't getting enough attention.

And I started being horrible to Ruby as well. Because I couldn't handle the way I was feeling. I'd occasionally give her a slap. Not especially hard, but certainly with enough force to send her into a crying fit that would require my parents to spend hours tending to her. I would hide her toys. Even break them on occasion. I did anything that would make her cry for practically the whole day.

I was a little shit for the two years Ruby was alive. It's one of those things that has stayed with me all this time.

I guess the meanest thing I did was ignore her. That was usually reserved for when I was feeling most spiteful. I would simply pretend that she didn't exist. I would pretend that she was invisible or something. No matter what she did, whether she wanted me to play with her or watch something together, I would just turn my head and act as though she wasn't there.

10

Jordan turns his wrist to show his tally mark tattoo. Two additional figures scored. The ink has a greenish tint, made all the more pronounced against a red patch of skin even darker than the surrounding sunburn.

"Does this look healthy to you guys?" he asks while scratching.

The three of us take a look and nod.

"Does it hurt?" Caleb asks.

Jordan shakes his head. "Not really, no."

"I wouldn't worry," I add, gazing far into the distance through my sunglasses.

I'm trying not to think about the fact that we'll be going home soon.

Ewan clears his throat. "Did you go back to that same tattoo place to get those new marks?"

"Yeah," Jordan responds. "It's like I'm on first name terms with the guy."

"What is his name?" Ewan asks.

"I don't know," Jordan shrugs. "I don't really care either."

We're at the harbour. The gleaming white façades of the old town are behind us, just over our shoulder. Not far from where I spent that night with Emma.

The outline of the garish beach bar is visible to my left.

There are around fifty of us waiting for this boat to show. We're dispersed in small pockets loitering around the harbour. There are snatched conversations. Sunglasses are fixed to phone screens. People are nursing hangovers. Heavy comedowns. Everybody is dressed in beachwear. Snippets of exposed flesh reveal either a bronzed glow or flaking sunburn, with nothing seemingly in between.

It's around midday. The sun beats down hard. It's impossibly humid, like you can't properly fill your lungs each time you open your mouth to breathe.

Nobody seems to mind though. The sky is clear blue. So is the sea.

The Heat of the Summer

And I guess that's all that matters.

We seem to be the only people out. There are a few locals taking shelter under the canopies of the bars and restaurants over the road, sitting down at tables with cold drinks and coffees and newspapers scattered in front of them, all looking over in silence.

But that's about it.

The small fishing boats and trawlers tied to the pier bob under the pressure of the soft-rolling waves. There's a persistent shushing, the sound of water lapping against the hulls of the old boats. Gulls squawk.

The picture is calm. Serene.

I'm not sure what we're talking about to fill the time. I give occasional grunts to whatever the lads say and it appears to suffice. No follow-up questions or need to elaborate. It suits me fine.

Ewan and Caleb both laugh at something Jordan says.

I do the same.

This all probably lasts for about fifteen, twenty minutes, until the boat arrives. It's noticeable on the horizon at first as a looming black shadow tearing across the crystalline surface. The noise of synthetic beats through the giant speakers craning from the deck becomes audible, bursting the quiet. "Ladbroke Grove" by AJ Tracey.

Everyone looks over, the locals bewildered.

The boat stops around half a mile from the harbour. The music cuts momentarily. There's a moment of terse calm before a deep, clear voice instantly recognisable as K-OS's sounds through the speakers.

"YO, IT'S A PANDEMONIUM SET. MOTHERFUCKING K-OS HERE LIVE AND DIRECT. YOU FUCKING FEEL ME, PEOPLE?"

A polite cheer ripples through the harbour. As though we're somehow inhibited in the daytime.

"YEAH, I'LL BE FUCKING ANGRY IF I FIND OUT ANY ONE OF YOU HAS BEEN TO SLEEP. NO FUCKING TIME FOR THAT SHIT. SAVE IT FOR WHEN

YOU'RE BACK HOME HATING YOUR LIFE."

The boat pulls up at one of the free bays. We climb the ladder in single file and arrive on deck to cheers and excited whoops from the Pandemonium girls, all of whom are sun-kissed with flowing blonde hair and bleached smiles. One inspects our tickets. Another hands each of us a slush drink which tastes of vodka and watermelon.

I look around the deck. Try to see if Crystal is on board.

K-OS leans over from the top deck as the boat fills up. He flashes a wide grin and adjusts his sunglasses and cuts the music and then grabs a microphone. His voice compels our attention.

"WELCOME ABOARD THE ORCA, FUCKERS, ABOUT TO SET SAIL ON THE HIGH SEAS. YOU EVER SEEN CAPTAIN PHILLIPS? THAT FUCKING SOMALI BROTHER? YO, I'M THE FUCKING CAPTAIN HERE. I'M GIVING ORDERS TO GET FUCKED UP. YOU ALL FUCKING FEEL ME? WHAT I SAY FUCKING GOES ABOARD THIS FUCKING BOAT. AND WHAT HAPPENS AT SEA STAYS AT FUCKING SEA. DON'T YOU DARE FUCKING FORGET THOSE TWO FUCKING RULES TODAY."

We sail further and further from the harbour, further and further from the island until all that can be seen from any angle is an unbroken stretch of clear-blue sea.

My head feels fuzzy. The world's edges have softened so much that everything suddenly seems fun and I can't help but feel invincible with that pleasing buzz surging through my body. I find that all I can do is smile and laugh at everything going on around me.

God knows how many drinks I've had. MDMA. The smallest of small bumps of coke.

K-OS soundtracks the party with banger after banger and occasionally interjects with loud commands for us to keep on enjoying ourselves, to do whatever the hell we want. We're far away from dry land, he keeps reminding us. Far from home.

The Heat of the Summer

Whatever happens at sea stays at sea. It's a mantra he repeats until there's a point where I think everybody on board begins to think that it's a universally acknowledged truth. All kinds of shit is done in plain sight. Any pretence of discretion is abandoned as people kiss and play with each other and even fuck in dizzying plumes of smoke and jets of foam pumped from machines. Others puke their guts overboard before going back for more.

K-OS screams for everyone to keep going. Tells us we're too tame. That we can do a whole lot better. We have it in us to crank things up another couple of notches.

Fun and games, he says over and over.

And that's exactly how it all feels.

I briefly wonder what Emma would have made of this if she were still here.

A plane flies overhead.

"Be Someone" blares through the huge speakers and a fleeting thought of that first night out here enters my head. When none of this seemed possible. Back when I hoped I'd be able to get away from reality but was worried that it would somehow find a way of creeping up on me. The way it always seems to whenever I let myself think I've found some kind of peace.

I'm really enjoying myself.

I really like it out here.

—

Night starts to fall and the boat turns around and heads back towards the harbour. There's disappointment on board at the news that the party is ending, but K-OS gets on the microphone and tells us all he's sorry but he has to DJ all night at Pandemonium. Because you can rest when you're dead, he says. He tells us that if we truly are hardcore, then we will all be down at the club that evening to crank things up a notch.

The boat picks up speed. I position myself by the railings with my arms dangling over the side. I keep my head turned right, away from the direction we are heading. I look out towards the horizon.

—

"Luke, are you coming with us?" Caleb calls out to me as I disembark the boat, halfway down the ladder.

The party is over. I'm the last to leave the boat. Everybody else has started to make their way towards the Strip.

The neon throb emanating from the clubs looms in the background. A strange effect enhanced against the backdrop of a purpling evening sky. A fluorescent rainbow arcing over the terracotta-tiled old town roofs.

Jordan and Ewan are waiting impatiently for me outside one of the bars across the street. Caleb is still ambling around the harbour, I think sensing that I'm reluctant to leave.

There's a clean-up operation on board the boat. The Pandemonium girls are busy filling black bin bags with rubbish. A couple of stocky guys dressed in tight-fitting Pandemonium T-shirts who I didn't notice on board earlier disconnect speakers and lug them down to the lower portion of the deck as K-OS leans against the railings and thumbs his phone.

I look down at Caleb, standing roughly halfway between the boat and the bar where Jordan and Ewan are waiting.

"I'll catch you all up," I shout over. "I think I left my wallet on board. I'll text you later to see where you are."

Caleb nods. He wanders back over to Jordan and Ewan, both busy tapping their phones. The three begin walking towards the Strip without exchanging a word.

I wait a few moments for them to merge with the crowd following the gradual curve of the beach over to the right. Until I'm unable to pick them out with any great confidence and they just become another set of anonymous bodies.

I climb back up the ladder and step back on deck.

Nobody on board acknowledges my presence. The Pandemonium girls continue picking up rubbish. The big guys carry on heaving speakers and sound equipment. I'm allowed to slide over to the top deck, where K-OS is pacing

The Heat of the Summer

from one end to the other engrossed in his phone.

The shot of confidence that comes with being pissed suddenly evaporates. My mouth goes dry. That familiar tightness in my chest returns at the worst possible moment.

K-OS glances up from his phone as though scenting me. He stares from across the top level with his lips pursed, his sunglasses hiding his expression.

"You okay, kid?" he asks.

"Yeah," I respond, nodding before a lengthy pause. "Look, I just wanted to say you were amazing today. Some of those tunes you played today were out of this world, man."

K-OS is quiet. Maintains his focus.

"Yeah."

Silence.

Waves roll against the boat. The far-off noise of cars.

"You DJ at Pandemonium, don't you?"

"What is it you want, kid? Are you after anything? Is this conversation going anywhere? Or are you just wanting to suck my dick or something?"

"Sorry?"

"Put it this way," he adds. "If you've got nothing important to say, you may as well just get off this boat. Because you're wasting my time here, kid."

I stare past K-OS, fixate for a moment on the whitewashed stone façades. Try to figure out what to say next. What I even hoped to achieve by initiating this conversation.

"A job," I eventually manage.

"What?"

"A job," I repeat in a tougher voice. "Do you think it would be possible if I..."

The sight of his face creasing into a frown throws me off for a moment.

"...if I could get a job at Pandemonium? I'll take anything. Literally anything."

K-OS sucks the inside of his cheeks. He shakes his head

and keeps his dark stare zeroed in on me.

"I don't think so, kid. Being out here isn't for everyone. I've seen people lose their minds because they couldn't handle it. Believe me." He looks me up and down and then shakes his head a second time. "Nah. No way."

Strains of that old song "Move Ya Body" drift up from the harbour. A car slows to a stop. The engine's purr cuts with the crank of a handbrake locking. The song fades.

It's the unexpected quiet that prompts K-OS to peer over the edge of the boat.

I angle my head over the side to see the same silver convertible that I caught a glimpse of outside Pandemonium in the early hours of this morning. The car door slams shut. A trim, tanned girl with dirty-blonde hair, dressed in denim shorts and a white tank-top saunters around to the passenger side. She leans back against the car with her arms folded and her lips clenched, glancing upwards at the boat through a pair of Wayfarer sunglasses.

Crystal.

K-OS turns his head back in my direction and goes to step past me.

"Sorry, kid. My ride's here."

"Is that Crystal down there?" I ask.

The question catches him by surprise. He stops dead and pushes his sunglasses further up the ridge of his nose—what must be a weird tic of sorts—and sights me puzzled.

"You know Crystal?"

"Yeah," I tell him.

He nods several times in response. Stares me down.

"She's a great girl," he says. "Real team player."

"Yeah. She is."

"How do you know her?"

I shrug. "Just from the club. Small talk and stuff, really."

"Has she said anything to you?"

"What? About a job?"

"Depends," he says, stroking his chin. "She said anything that interested you?"

I shake my head. "Just mentioned something about a job in passing. That was it, really."

"Right," K-OS answers.

"Yeah," I say, trying to sound confident. "She said you carried some sway at Pandemonium. That it might be worth talking to you. I'm hoping to stay out here a little longer, you see. I told her I want to carry on the party. I'm not ready to go home."

K-OS snorts. "Yeah, kid, I know the feeling," His mouth parts in a razor-sharp grin. "Fucking Neverland out here, you get me? Know what I'm saying, kid?"

K-OS again looks past me to stare far off into the distance. He moves his lips slowly to repeat the word "Neverland" under his breath. A stiff smile breaks. He then nods and tunes back into his surroundings, looking me over while pushing his sunglasses up the ridge of his nose again.

"But," he says. "I'm not sure why Crystal would tell you to look me up when she has a direct line to the boss man himself."

A car horn honks.

K-OS and I both look over the edge of the top deck to see Crystal back at the wheel of the silver convertible. She raises a hand and motions for K-OS to hurry up. Her frustration is evident even from this vantage point. She sighs, slumps back against the leather upholstery.

K-OS turns back to me. "Sorry, kid. Got to go. This bitch has got no patience." He glances down at Crystal and then returns his attention to me. "Look, I don't really have much of a say in the hiring and firing at Pandemonium. My expertise lies elsewhere, you get me? But I'm actually meeting the big guy tomorrow morning. I can't promise anything, but if you drop by the club you might find yourself in luck."

K-OS shifts past me, still talking.

"The big guy's name is Lucio. I'll put in a word for you and I'm sure Crystal will have already whispered something in his ear. But you need to up your game tomorrow, kid.

The Heat of the Summer

None of this pussyfooting shit you came up here with at first. Lucio likes them fearless, see. No nervousness. No hesitation. Not a shred of doubt. I'm talking balls out, kid. Balls fucking out. You tell him why you want a job so bad. You tell him you'll do anything to warrant that shot. And then, like I say, you may find yourself getting lucky in becoming another lost boy."

K-OS forces a laugh after his closing line. He steps down onto the lower deck and moves through the crowd of girls still busy cleaning up and then descends two or three rungs down the ladder. He pauses to give me one final look back.

"See you tomorrow, kid," he calls as his lips curl into another wide smile. "Well... maybe."

—

I don't bother going out.

I've had a few texts from the boys asking where I am. I reply that I'm feeling a little sick. The messages I get in response are typically full of abuse, predictably branding me a pussy.

Jordan has tried to call a couple of times. I've let the phone ring out and stuck it on silent in the hope that he will soon give up.

I'm back at the room, tucked up in bed. The mattress is hard against my back, the feeling excruciating, having sobered up.

I'm lying in the dark hoping that I'll somehow fall asleep. A faint white glow rising from the Strip lingers in the far corner of the room, noticeable through the thin billowing curtains, the balcony doors slid open to allow some fresh air to circulate. Electronic sounds pass in and out.

I try to picture staying out here. How different my life would be.

11

I'm up early. Around 7:30. Not that I slept much anyway. I just lay in the dark with my eyes closed and pretended to be asleep as Ewan came in and made a real racket getting into bed, tripping over his own feet and dragging his body across the dirty floor before collapsing on the mattress.

I stare at myself in the bathroom mirror. I look physically tired with bags under my bloodshot eyes and a colourless complexion.

But I try to push past this. I try not to let it bother me.

It's typically hot and humid outside. The early morning sun hangs low in the cloudless blue sky.

I grab a small cup of coffee from a McDonald's that's a five minute walk from the hotel in the hope that it will sharpen me up. I take a series of long, slow sips, veering onto the Strip.

The place is dead. No people. No music. No blinking neon lights. A delicate breeze comes out of nowhere and pushes litter around the pavements. The low scratch of polystyrene takeaway containers against tarmac meshes with birdsong. A seagull swoops down a few yards in front of me and picks at a puddle of congealed vomit. Several others peck at a mound of chicken wings and chips from an overturned cardboard bucket. The breeze kicks up into a swirling gust which rattles the length of the narrow concrete corridor to create an eerie tuneless whistle.

I make it to Pandemonium. The doors are wide open. I take a few nervous steps and stop under the threshold, ready to coach myself down the tunnel.

It soon becomes apparent that it's a completely different proposition during the day. The light from outside permeates the inside of the passageway to offer a clear sight of the club the whole way down, where I'm able to make out some kids dressed in black Pandemonium T-shirts cleaning up. The clank of my footsteps against the metal floor echoing around the tunnel prompts a tanned kid with short black hair and a sleeve tattoo mopping the floor at the tunnel's mouth to look towards me.

"Is K-OS around?" I ask him.

The kid grunts a response and points in the direction of the bar.

I step through the crowd of kids cleaning up, all of whom look around my age or slightly older at a push. I head over to the bar, where a couple of tanned girls with short black hair are cleaning the fridges and emptying the drip trays. There's a small doorway around six feet high and three feet wide dividing the row of spirit bottles fixed to the wall.

I ask the girls if K-OS is through there. They both nod their heads without saying a word, each wearing the same jaded expression.

I walk down a narrow dusty corridor with a cracked ceiling which slopes down towards a red door lit by a naked bulb. The corridor walls are painted burgundy and adorned with framed photographs of the club from different summers stretching back even before I was born. The general tone of each photograph is the same, with raucous partygoers packed tight, bathed in a rainbow light show. I look at the sea of ecstatic faces from the 1990s and early 2000s. Everyone wide-eyed and delirious, radiating unmistakable joy. All young and carefree. Boys and girls pressed close, staring down the lens, lost in a single euphoric moment.

I stop outside the red door. I find that I'm stooping, such is the feeling that the ceiling is on top of me. I raise my fist and knock.

A gruff voice comes from inside. "Yeah?"

I slowly push open the door and peer inside to see K-OS sitting at a table strewn with papers and disposable coffee cups and stacks of money, along with a single packet of cigarettes. There's another guy opposite him dressed in a neatly-pressed immaculate white shirt. The man turns around at the dry squeak of the metal hinges. We lock eyes for a split second.

The driver of the silver convertible. The guy who picked Crystal up from outside the club the other night.

And, sure enough, I glance past the two men to see Crystal sitting cross-legged on an old black leather couch set against the back wall. Her left arm is perched on the armrest and she holds her phone in her right hand, ceasing texting for a moment to give me a listless look. She sighs and runs a hand back through her dirty-blonde hair and then lowers her head to resume tapping at the screen.

K-OS smiles. He's still wearing sunglasses despite the room being dark and dingy.

"Hey, morning, kid," he says, beckoning me inside. He looks back at the guy in the white shirt sitting opposite. "Lucio, man, this is the kid I was talking about. Came up to me yesterday after the boat party asking about a job here."

The white-shirted guy, Lucio, swivels in his chair to eye me up and down.

"This kid?" he asks, turning back to K-OS.

"Yeah, this kid, man," K-OS nods. He extends one of his bulging arms and pulls out a foldaway steel chair beside him. "Come here, kid, take a seat. Let's see if we can work something out, huh?

I take the offered seat.

"This is the kid you said was golden, man?" Lucio sneers. There's a noticeable foreign inflection to his speech. Either Spanish or Portuguese. "I don't know, K. I usually get a gut feeling about these kinds of things. He doesn't look like he has it in him to me."

I interrupt, going against my gut instinct. "I've worked in a bar before. I know how things work."

Lucio glowers, returns to K-OS.

"This is what I mean, K," Lucio says. "Kids think it's all one long party out here. They think they know how it's going to be. And then they run a fucking mile when they realise how hard they have to work."

He narrows his eyes at me, lifts a finger.

"Firstly, kid, you're a fucking ghost in this room, as far as I'm concerned. Don't say a word. Don't move a muscle. Nothing without prior instruction." He pauses and raises a second finger. "And second, never make the mistake of thinking I'm stupid, kid. You really think you're the first person to come to me asking for a job? You're nothing new to me, kid. I've lost count of the number of kids your age coming in here to ask for a job after exchanging pleasantries with one of the fuck-heads already working here. They think shit like that gives them a way in. A lot of kids like you have such a good time out here that they don't want the party to end. And that's part of the problem, you see. They think it's all going to be one long party out here. They have no idea about the hard work involved. They don't care. And then they run away scared when it eventually dawns on them. They can't cope with the demands of this place."

Out of the corner of my eye I notice K-OS stare at Lucio through his sunglasses. The tap of Crystal texting fills the silence.

Lucio picks up, stretching for a cigarette. "See, kid, and that's the thing here. Nothing good out here comes free and easy. Yeah, no doubt you can have a great time. The time of your life, in fact. But you've got to work hard for it. So forgive me, kid, but I've seen this movie before. I know how it goes. And you've got that same look about you as I've seen in countless other kids who have come and gone."

"I'm not scared of hard work," I answer, purging my voice of any nervousness. "Trust me. Please."

"Look, Lucio," K-OS interrupts, "I've got to admit, I wasn't sure about the kid at first. But he's shown he's serious by coming down here. I tried to size him last night and he didn't back down. Credit. I know he doesn't look much, but he's got front and that's at least something we can work with. I can't think of too many people who would approach me after a show the way he did, or would come down here and fight his corner like this. He's got game, no question."

Lucio rolls the cigarette between his fingers. "K, man, you know as well as I do that the hard work I'm talking about isn't just confined to the club."

"Yeah."

"Trust. Loyalty," Lucio says, arching forward. "They're their own separate burdens."

"Agreed."

My eyes flit back and forth between the two guys.

"Because you know we can't take any unnecessary risks right now," Lucio adds. "Things are tight."

"Yeah," K-OS nods.

Lucio sighs. "So, all things considered, where are we on this? I know you're vouching for the kid here, but I'm going to need some convincing, to be honest. There's too much going on right now without me having to worry about whether we can get some kid up to speed when we may need to get our game faces on soon."

K-OS nods again.

Lucio places the cigarette between his lips. "Things are tight right now," he repeats. "You know that, don't you, K?"

"Yeah, I feel you, man. I know what's going down," K-OS answers, his lips parting in a wry smile. "Something wicked this way comes, huh?"

Lucio gets to his feet. He motions for K-OS to stand.

"I'm going outside for a smoke," Lucio announces. "We'll talk about this in private, K."

Both men exit the office to leave me alone with Crystal. The creak of the door opening and then closing fails to distract her from her phone.

She remains quiet. Doesn't engage with me at all.

Completely bored, I'm left to study my surroundings.

It's a cramped space. No windows. Wall-to-wall clutter. There's a large oak desk set against the mint green breezeblock wall with an old dusty computer monitor and office stationery chaotically scattered. A tower of stuffed ring binders and dog-eared manila folders. There's a large safe in one corner of the room adjacent to the couch Crystal is sat on. A water cooler and a fridge opposite.

My mind wanders. About the building itself. The weird layout of the place. How nothing fits. The imposing exterior and the compact club area. The winding tunnels and shrinking corridors. More a fairground funhouse than a serious, practical design.

The place is so confusing it's hard to get an exact picture in my head.

I angle my body to face Crystal. "You okay?"

She glances up from her phone. "Sorry?"

"You okay?"

She shrugs, resumes tapping at the screen. "Yeah."

The distant noise of hoovering from down the other end of the corridor.

"You up to much today?" I enquire.

"What are you doing here?"

"Excuse me?"

"What are you doing here?" she repeats.

I pause. Smile.

"I'm looking for a job. Like I've said."

"No," she glares, setting her phone down beside her. "What are you really doing here? What exactly are you hoping to achieve by being here and getting involved in this sort of thing, Luke?"

"You remember my name?" I say, surprised.

She nods. "Yeah. I do. Of course I do. I'm not a fucking goldfish. I may look like I don't know what's going on but never make the mistake of assuming that to be the case—"

The approach of footsteps outside induces silence. The door opens. Lucio and K-OS both enter, stand over me.

"Up, kid," Lucio growls.

I get to my feet.

Lucio offers a handshake. Hard. Firm.

"Welcome aboard, kid," he says, glancing past me to tip his head at K-OS. "You've got this man here to thank."

Lucio releases his grip. I turn around, fall straight into a clumsy hug from K-OS. He taps my cheek before pushing me away, playfully punching my shoulder.

"Don't let me down here, kid," K-OS tells me sternly.

"No, K-OS. Absolutely not."

A pat on the back.

"You go and get your stuff together and come back here this afternoon. Crystal will take care of you," he adds.

12

I arrive back at the hotel.

It's a relief knowing I'll be seeing this place for the last time.

Ewan is packing his folded clothes into his suitcase. Jordan and Caleb are both sitting on my bed with their cases zipped shut and stood upright on the floor next to them.

Jordan gets to his feet. "Luke, where the hell have you been? The shuttle bus is coming to pick us up in twenty minutes and all of your shit is still in the wardrobe."

I head into the bathroom and start packing my toiletries into my washbag. Jordan's voice travels through into the room. My name repeated over and over.

There's frustration in his voice, discernible anger rising each time I fail to respond.

I step back into the room and toss the washbag onto my bed, landing inches from Jordan's thigh. I drag my suitcase out from underneath the plastic patio table still littered with beer cans and nos canisters and all kinds of other shit.

Jordan keeps repeating my name as I move back and forth from wardrobe to suitcase, carrying my clothes and picking up anything that is mine from the floor.

"Luke, have you fucking gone deaf or something?"

"I hear you, mate," I say without looking up.

"Then how about fucking answering me?" he snarls. "Why did you just wander off this morning without saying anything? We've been worried about you. Worried that you'd miss the shuttle."

I tip my head to each of the boys. First Jordan. Then Ewan. And finally Caleb. "I didn't say anything to any of you because it was none of your business where I was. It didn't concern a single one of you."

"You know, I wish you'd stop being such a fucking weirdo," Jordan mutters, rolling his eyes. His tone picks up. "But, okay, whatever. It doesn't matter now. Just hurry up so we don't miss this shuttle bus."

"I'm not going," I say in a calm, quiet voice.
"What are you talking about? Of course you're getting on the bus. Fucking weirdo."
I shake my head. "No. I'm not."
Jordan steps over to me. "Don't talk shit. Of course you're coming."
I glance upwards. Meet his stare. "I'm not messing around, Jordan. I've told you, I'm not going to the airport with you guys."
I continue packing.
"Jesus fucking Christ, you've been acting weird this whole trip, you know? Didn't that pep talk I gave you at the beach a couple of days ago have any effect? You go off sulking and develop some strange infatuation with a fat girl, blow her off suddenly, and then you decide to go for an early morning wander to nowhere in particular and worry us all sick that we're going to miss our bus to the airport. Can't you just be fucking normal for once?"
"Not that it concerns you, but I had a job interview. And that's the reason why I won't be getting on the bus with you all," I reply. "Because I got the job."
"A job?" Ewan asks.
"Yeah. A job."
"Bollocks," Jordan sneers.
"No," I respond, glancing over my shoulder at Ewan and Caleb. "I'm telling the truth. I've got a job. It means I'll be staying out here for a little bit longer."
"He doesn't have a job. He's bullshitting us." Jordan then stops to look at Ewan and Caleb, jabbing a finger in my direction. "Can't you dickheads tell he's taking the piss? Why else would he be packing? It's obvious. Because he's coming to the airport with us. He's just trying to make us all look like idiots. As if anybody out here would offer him a job. My bet is that he picked up another fatty somewhere and fucked her."
I throw the washbag and the last of my clothes into the suitcase. I turn again to Jordan, scan his hulking frame. "The

reason I'm packing is because the owner of the club told me to get my stuff together and meet him back there this afternoon."

"Oh yeah? Which club?"

"Pandemonium."

"How did you swing that?" Caleb asks, tapping his phone.

"Just through talking," I shrug. "I had a chat with the DJ from the boat party yesterday. I think he took a shine to me—"

"He's probably grooming you," Jordan interrupts. "Likes his guys young, tight and inexperienced."

I ignore him. "And one of the girls who works there—Crystal—I've been getting along pretty well with her. She said I'd be a good fit for the place and that she'd put in a good word for me."

"You like this girl, mate?" Ewan pipes up.

"Well, we're just friends at the minute," I shrug. "But I think we could end up as more. I honestly do."

Jordan snorts. "So you haven't fucked this girl yet?"

"What? Oh no, not yet. It might take time. But I think we'll get there. Honestly."

Caleb is still tapping at his phone. "What's her name? Crystal? Which one was she again?"

"The tall tanned girl with the dirty-blonde hair. Great tits."

Caleb screws his face. "All of those girls look the same in that place."

"Hey, she's not taller than you, is she, Luke?" Jordan sniggers. "You're not going to have to borrow her heels to go in for a kiss, are you?"

I ignore Jordan to look straight at Caleb. "Yeah, man, but Crystal's the best of them, you know what I mean? The girl who gave us those free shot vouchers the other night. Remember? Can you picture her?"

Caleb shakes his head. "No."

Jordan rages. "Bullshit. So you've suddenly gone from snaring a pig to bagging the hottest girl working at the club?

You're full of shit, Luke. Always have been, always will be. You must think we're fucking stupid."

"She was the girl you actually commented on when we were queuing to get into the club," I respond, pointing at Jordan. "'Jesus, what a woman' is what you said, if I remember rightly. And she's interested in me, man. She wants me. How about that, huh?"

"Bullshit," Jordan repeats, red-faced. He kicks the frame of the bed, begins pointing at me. "She'll be stringing you along for something. I don't know what, but it will be for something. If she's as hot as you say she is, I guarantee she'll have an ulterior motive. Girls like that don't get involved in charity."

I shake my head.

Jordan goes on. "Thinking about this a little, I suspect you've got your hopes up. Girls like that are paid to make eyes at people. You probably got over-excited speaking to a whore like that and somehow managed to bullshit a job. Probably out of pity. That's what I think, anyway."

I narrow my eyes. "Don't call her a whore. You don't know a single thing about her."

Jordan smirks. He lowers his head to mine. Forehead pressed to forehead. "And I bet you don't either."

I push back.

"Why don't you just shut your mouth for once, Jordan? Why don't you just give it a rest? You've always had too much to say for yourself. I don't think I'm alone here in saying you've fucking ruined this holiday with your non-stop sniping and your stupid little jibes. You're just a fucking bully, you know that?"

"Feeling fucking brave, aren't you, kid? Did that pig Emma hand you back your balls before she flew home?"

Something happens. I'm not sure what exactly.

It's a feeling which overcomes me in an instant. Before I can begin to comprehend it. The best way I can describe it—possibly even the only way—is that it's like a sudden crack of white-hot lightning.

The Heat of the Summer

A blinding flash.

What feels like an out of body experience.

I find that I'm watching myself from the ceiling, watching myself sprawled on top of Jordan, who is spread flat across Ewan's bed.

I have no idea how this happened.

I assume that I caught Jordan by surprise. I must have. Because it's the only way I would be able to force him off his feet and backwards onto the bed.

Jordan lies completely vulnerable, waving his hands in some desperate attempt at protecting himself. One of my hands is bunched around the neck of his T-shirt. The other is sending punch after punch into the centre of his face. His nose has burst open. His blood flecks my cheeks. My eyes are glazed watching his bloodied face collapse in a sunken mess.

It takes Ewan and Caleb a while to react. Both of them wear the same stunned expression. It's only when a gurgled whimper leaves Jordan's lips that they react. They throw their arms around me and pull me back, throw me sideways onto the other bed.

It's at this point that I find I'm back inside myself.

Ewan's fingers dig into my shoulders, keeping me in place while Caleb rushes to Jordan with soaked toilet paper.

I'm exhausted, unable to do anything but gawp at the sight of Jordan rolling from one side to the other on top of a bloodied bedsheet. He screams and wails. Turns away from Caleb tending to his exploded nose. Tears stream.

Ewan says something to me which doesn't sink in.

Jordan's howls overlay all surrounding noise. He stumbles to his feet assisted by Caleb, who takes an arm around his shoulder. He staggers forward a few clumsy steps, revealing that his T-shirt has been ripped down the middle in a jagged V-pattern.

I look down at the floor embarrassed, belatedly realising that I'm holding a torn piece of T-shirt in my blood-stained hand.

Caleb heaves Jordan over to the door and says something to Ewan about getting the cases together and meeting him down in the lobby.

Ewan agrees.

Caleb then adds something else about seeing whether Jordan should go to hospital. Whether he'll even be able to fly in such a condition.

Ewan nods.

The door shuts.

Ewan gets to his feet and gathers the suitcases. He wheels them out into the hallway one by one. He takes one last look at me before leaving the room.

"Are you going to be okay?" Ewan asks me.

I don't make eye contact. In the corners of my eyes I feel tears form, which I struggle to stem.

I gulp. Respond with a feeble nod.

"Remember to hand your key back in at reception, okay?"

"Yeah," I manage.

There are a few seconds of silence, during which Ewan lets out a long sigh and takes a last look around the room before resetting his attention on me. Presumably in the hope that I'll glance up and return his stare.

But I'm really not in the mood. I just want to forget about all of this. Pretend it never happened.

Start afresh.

Ewan hovers in the doorway. He clears his throat.

"Look. Take care of yourself, okay?"

I nod.

"See you around, mate," I mumble.

"Yeah."

Ewan closes the door.

An uneasy quiet fills the room.

I can't hold it in any longer.

I start to cry.

I fall onto my back and cover my face with my hands and bawl. My whole body convulses as I pull myself into the foetal position.

The Heat of the Summer

It's while wiping some tears that I notice the state of my right knuckle. My left hand clamps tight around my right fist, bringing it up to my face. I turn it slowly from side to side and carefully inspect the peeling skin and the swelling, the discolouration, the stained residue of blood and tissue all meshing together. A monotonous ache sets in.

The tears stop suddenly and unexpectedly. I take several deep, calming breaths and force myself to sit upright.

13

The sun is at its highest point. The dead centre of an unending bright blue canvas.

The heat throbs. As it only ever seems to do out here. As though it's the only thing it can do. Not even a hint of a breeze to relieve the tension.

The Strip is gradually filling. There are a few small hungover groups at tables on the terraces of different bars nursing whatever hair of the dog takes their fancy. A couple of spaced-out stragglers wander through the previous night's debris. Some fast food outlets are opening.

I meet Crystal outside Pandemonium just after midday. She's propped up against the closed front entrance with a sullen demeanour. Her shoulders are slumped. She taps at her phone. Adjusts her Wayfarers.

Some manual workers unload large crates from a parked lorry and take them into the club through a service entrance at the side.

"Lucio and K-OS not around?" I ask Crystal.

She shakes her head without looking up from her phone. "Not their concern. They've got other things to worry about."

We load my belongings into the back of the silver convertible parked at the rear of the club and begin the journey to wherever. I keep my eyes fixed outside of the car the whole time. The scene around us dissolves from that of a tourist trap to a patch of grey apartment buildings at the foot of some brooding amber hills.

I try to make conversation. Pointless small talk. Hollow pleasantries.

Crystal remains unresponsive, however. Her gaze remains directed at the road ahead stretching out for miles.

We park outside one of the buildings. I grab my things and follow her inside. We take the lift up to the fifth floor.

I again try to force a conversation.

"Any plans for this afternoon?"

Crystal stares at the rusting metal lift panels.

The doors ping open at the fifth floor. She gives me a lazy look.

"Sorry?"

"You got any plans this afternoon?"

She shrugs. "Not much."

Crystal leads me down a narrow peach-coloured corridor which smells of damp. There's an eerie quiet apart from the roll of my suitcase wheels over the tiled floor and a low crackle emanating from the ceiling bulbs.

She stops outside a pea-green door, the frame of which is splintered and chipped. The dull metal numbers read 579. Crystal raps hard on the door.

Muffled music comes from inside. Some rap or R&B.

A distinct shuffling sound follows. A voice calls out. A loud clattering noise followed by the rattle of keys. The door opens and we're greeted by a tall mixed-race kid with his hair bunched together at the back. He appears a few years older than me—maybe twenty-two or twenty-three—slightly gaunt with smooth facial features and a pair of bloodshot eyes flitting back and forth between me and Crystal. He gives her a thin smile, scratches at his bare pigeon chest. The only item of clothing he's wearing is a pair of grey tracksuit bottoms. He proceeds to stuff both hands down the front, leaning against the door frame.

"Hey," he says.

The flash of a gold tooth as he opens his mouth. A light Scottish accent.

The guy's right eye twitches.

Crystal gestures at me. "This is Luke. Your new roommate."

He lifts an eyebrow. "The other one gone for good, then?"

Crystal shrugs. "I guess so. It's not as if Lucio would ever tell me anything, is it?"

The guy nods. A grave expression forms. He then opens the door wider and stands to one side to welcome me in.

"Nice to meet you, man. I'm Ryan," he says, clasping my hand.

"Yeah. Same."

I glance down at his long toenails and then back up at his face, faintly marked with acne scars. The guy twitches a second time. He carefully rubs his hands together and forces a smile.

The flat itself is pretty basic. Open-plan. The scale of degradation exposed in plain sight. Dried mud marks the tiled floor and the whitewashed walls. The kitchen is positioned to my right, where I see a sink full of filthy dishes and a draining board caked with lime scale. Food stains and crumbs are scattered the length of the cracked laminate worktop, curving out into a breakfast bar topped with torn cereal boxes and an open pack of bacon. There's a small circular dining table to my left packed high with dirty crumpled clothes. A living area strewn with beer bottles and crisp packets and fast food containers is further ahead, where a recliner and a tired couch face a TV screen showing a paused FIFA game. A scratched coffee table fills the space between furniture and appliances. At the far end of the flat are two closed doors, which I assume must be the bedrooms.

It's from that general direction I realise the music is coming. What sounds like a Run the Jewels track.

The flat stinks of pot. A lit joint in an ashtray on top of the coffee table.

Ryan turns his back to us and walks over to the living area and sits down on the couch and then takes a puff of the joint. He picks up a PS5 controller and continues his game.

"So, this is you, Luke," Crystal says.

The air conditioning hums in the background. Cool air hits me moving into the living area.

Ryan hits pause and takes a long toke.

"You play?" he asks, motioning at the screen with the joint clamped between his fingers.

"Yeah."

"Any good?"

"I'm okay."

The Heat of the Summer

Ryan blows some smoke and hands me the second controller. His facial tic strikes. "Plenty of time to get better, man."

I bat an empty can of Coke and a scrunched burger wrapper from the couch to the floor and sit down next to Ryan.

I look at Crystal before the game restarts. She's motionless, slumped against the door frame. She stares straight past Ryan and me, lost in her thoughts.

"Well, have fun, boys," she says in a low voice.

She turns around. Leaves.

—

Hi, Mum, it's me. Look, I've got something to tell you. Please don't be mad ... What? ... No—Mum ... Mum ... Calm down, will you? Like I said, it's nothing bad, I just need you to listen to me and I need you to support my decision.

Basically, what it is—I won't be coming home today. I've decided to stay out here a little bit longer ... Mum ... Mum ... Mum ... Jesus-fucking-Christ, Mum, will you calm down? Just calm down ... I'm sorry for swearing, but I need you to stop screaming. I need you to listen to me ... Look, if you're not going to calm down, I'm going to hang up. I need you to calm down and hear me out.

Are you taking deep breaths? Are you calm? ... Okay, good. What it is—I've been offered a job out here for the rest of the summer and I've decided to take it ... What? ... It's nothing major, I'll just be working in this club out here, working behind the bar ... I just got talking to the owner one day and he seemed to like me and he offered me a summer job and, yeah, I took it ... Mum ... Mum ... You see, that's your problem, Mum, you're so untrusting. You always think the worst of people. You need to pull yourself together because you can't live your life like that.

Look, I'm sorry, I didn't mean that. I shouldn't have said it. I don't want to pick a fight over the phone, but I need you to back me up here. Have a look at things from my perspective. The weather is great, I've met so many amazing people and I'm having such a good time. Honestly, what is there for me at home? ... Yeah ... Yeah, I know—my family—but I'll be home in around a month or two or whatever. I'll see everybody then ... Okay, yeah, I know I have a job at Sainsbury's, but, honestly, the place isn't exactly going to go bankrupt if all of a sudden I decide not to show up for work one day, is it? I think they'll manage.

The thing I need you to appreciate, Mum, is that it's like I'm a different person out here. This place is doing me the world of good. I know you've been worried about me for ages—about my panic attacks and all of my anxieties and whether or not I'd fit in and make friends at university—but, honestly, I feel like I've really changed as a person out here. Trust me, when I get home, you'll see a new me. It's like I'm finally at ease with myself now. I feel comfortable in my own skin.

What? Yeah, don't be silly, Mum, of course I'll be coming home. I'll be home before I start uni. I'm not going to throw away everything I've worked so hard for just for some summer job. It's just all about new experiences and living my life—making the most of things while I still can ... Of course, it'll be great to see you and everyone else ... Grandad? Is he—? ... Look, I'm sure it's nothing... He gets that way sometimes, doesn't he? ... Can you pass on my love, please, Mum?

What's that? ... A girl? What girl? ... Oh, yeah, right—Emma ... Yeah, it didn't really work out in the end ... Aw, don't feel bad. It was just one of those things. Stuff like that happens, you know? Besides, I've met someone else ... What? ... No, look, I'll have to tell you about her some other time. There's stuff I need to do. I'm a bit busy at the minute.

Look, Mum, I've really got to go. I'd love to talk longer, but I really can't... Of course I'll be in touch. I'll tell you more about what I'm up to. I'll keep you updated, I promise ... Yeah, I can't wait to see you either, Mum. Love you ...

The Heat of the Summer

Love you loads. And give my love to everyone back home … See you later… Bye.

14

I don't like to think about Ruby too much. As you can probably tell.

The memory of her feels like something I've been constantly trying to escape.

Everyone has told me I shouldn't feel guilty about what happened. That it wasn't my fault. It was just one of those things that can't be helped.

I don't know if that's genuinely how people feel or whether it's something they say to try to make me feel better. I get that there's good intentions behind their words, but it doesn't make a difference to how I feel.

It also ignores the fact that Ruby would still be here if I had looked after her better that day. If I had not been so careless. You can say whatever you like to try to excuse what happened—call it bad luck, a freak occurrence, the wrong place at the wrong time or whatever else—and maybe there is an element of truth to it, but it doesn't matter one little bit. It's happened. Nothing can change it. That's the long and short of it.

I realise that I was a kid myself. But it's no real excuse. I was her big brother. I was responsible for her safety.

Nobody can convince me of anything else.

It was my fault.

It was a warm day. Right on the cusp of summer. That time of year when the pleasant spring weather threatens to change into something more hostile.

It happened during the half-term break. I remember that clearly because I was off school and brimming with energy.

This was during my difficult phase. My relationship with Ruby was distinctly love-hate, even though I had definitely started warming to her a little. I sensed my parents were having issues based on the fact that they barely saw each other since moving into the new house and they hardly ever spoke when they did. The vastness of the house only seemed to emphasise the silence.

I wasn't shy in using their dissatisfaction to my advantage, to be totally honest. I often played one off against the other to get the things I wanted. Sweets and junk food. Additional screen time. A slightly later bedtime. It's not really something I'm proud of. But I can't pretend it didn't happen.

Dad's workload was intense at this point. He would typically arrive home long after my bedtime. I would sometimes hear them argue when I couldn't sleep. I would open the door slightly and poke my head around the frame so I could get a better listen. Sometimes it was hard to get a sense of what they were saying because there was a lot of swearing and the actual shouting tended to obscure the crux of the argument. I think it was mostly about Dad's working hours. I once heard Mum complain that he was late home and Dad angrily replied that the mortgage needed paying and then Mum responded by saying she never wanted to move in the first place. And I think that turned into a fight about Ruby. Both accused each other of not being careful.

I think Mum was unhappy about staying at home all the time. She was on sabbatical from work to help raise Ruby. It's not something Mum would admit now, but I'm sure she resented it at the time. I can recall my parents discussing the possibility of getting a nanny, but it was something Dad was dead against. I think he disliked the idea of someone from outside the family raising the baby. Mum asked Dad if it had crossed his mind to put his career on ice and he said that he earned more than her so shouldn't have to.

Mum was especially pissed off on the day it happened. Completely fried. I overheard her once try to put a positive spin on her situation by telling Dad that she would at least have an opportunity to write whenever the baby napped. But that was proving more difficult than expected. And she also had me being a nightmare to contend with. Even though I was more than capable of keeping myself entertained, I harangued her regardless, desperate for attention.

The Heat of the Summer

The picture of Mum red-faced and flustered with her hair stood on end that day is still vivid. She had managed to buy herself a modicum of peace and quiet by promising me some chicken dippers and chips even though it must only have been late morning at the time.

I was in the conservatory with Ruby. My mother was in the adjoining living room sprawled on the couch occasionally glancing at us over the pages of her book. I suspect she was happy to see that I was silent and still watching TV. Ruby was toddling by now, but she was quite happy in the far corner of the conservatory playing with some building blocks. The doors leading out into the garden were wide open, allowing fresh air to circulate through the house.

The phone rang. My eyes were glued to whatever I was watching. It's quite funny because I couldn't tell you with any certainty what the hell I had on the TV, but I'll always remember the ring of that phone.

I doubt it even registered at the time. There was no way I could conceive of how significant something so incidental could become. It's only later when you look back over things and begin pinpointing where and how they went wrong do you realise the full importance of every little thing on that day.

Mum folded the corner of her page and set down her book. She got up off the couch and went out into the hallway.

I was aware of Ruby still playing out of the corner of my eye.

Mum must have been on the phone for around five minutes. I'm not sure who she was talking to. I've never asked her.

It's irrelevant, I guess.

I remember the fire alarm made me jump. Its shrill noise blasted through the house. I heard my mother swear loudly down the phone. She ran along the hallway, through the morning room and into the kitchen.

I followed after her. The noise was giving me a headache. I kept my hands pressed tight over my ears to try to block it.

The Heat of the Summer

I could see plumes of black smoke billowing from the kitchen. I made my way through the morning room, coughing and spluttering. I pulled my T-shirt up over my mouth.

My mother's coughs undercut the alarm. I stood motionless in the kitchen doorway and watched Mum kneeling on top of the work surface, hunched over the blazing chip pan by the sink. She was wafting the flames with a tea towel, trying to quell the smoke. Cold water streamed into the sink basin. Mum strained her body towards the tap and wet the tea towel, wrung it out and threw it over the fire. She seized another tea towel that was balled up on the draining board and clambered to her feet using the window sill for support, stretching towards the fire alarm in the centre of the ceiling.

It was at this point Mum noticed me. She stared wide-eyed. She shouted something that I couldn't make out over the alarm.

I froze. Even though I had no clue what she was saying, I must have had a terrified look on my face. She kept screaming and pointing past me while trying to disperse the smoke with the tea towel in her other hand. I remember shaking my head, clamping my hands even tighter over my ears to the stage where I had lost feeling in them. I think I was screaming too, totally overcome by the chaos.

And all the while Mum kept screaming and pointing. Her expression was like nothing I'd ever seen before. Sheer terror. Mum's cries continued to be drowned out by the alarm until the noise suddenly cut after enough smoke had wafted through the open windows.

"The baby," Mum screeched in the quiet after the mayhem. "Why aren't you watching the baby?"

We found Ruby floating face down in the pond at the bottom of the garden.

The image of my mum jumping into the pond fully clothed and wading through the marsh and the algae to fish her out is still clear in my head.

I doubt it will ever be anything but.

I called 999 on the house phone and asked for an ambulance. The operator asked what had happened. I said my baby sister had fallen in our garden pond. The operator promised me that the ambulance would be as quick as possible. I thanked her and hung up.

I stood at the top of the embankment and watched on, aghast. Paralysed by how unreal it seemed.

Mum was slumped forward on her knees. She cradled Ruby while giving her the kiss of life. Tears cascaded down my mother's cheeks and trickled over the ashen-white face of my baby sister.

15

The last few weeks have been a whirlwind. A total blur.
I'm having a blast. I've never felt better.
I honestly mean it.
Whenever people asked me how I was in the past, I would often just pretend that I was okay. Say that I was enjoying myself. But there would always be this emptiness, this profound sadness I could never shift.
I guess I just learnt to live with it.
I mean, I wouldn't say I was completely miserable all of the time, but it was a feeling I was always conscious of.
I suspect it was what Jordan was talking about when he mentioned stuff about finding me inhibited or boring, or whatever else he used to say.
But none of that matters now. Jordan doesn't matter. He's in the past. A thousand or so miles away for good measure.
My head is clear now. I feel calm and relaxed. I'm genuinely happy for the first time in as far back as I can recall.
It's a non-stop party out here. There's always something going on. The island never sleeps, to borrow a phrase from K-OS.
I get giddy and light-headed just thinking about it all. A permanent high. I sometimes find myself overwhelmed trying to take everything in. Trying to process all that's happened to me.
I've learnt to go with the flow now. To simply take everything as it comes.
Because there's no point worrying about anything that's outside your control.
Just wake up and breathe easy and go with things depending on how they fall.
The days out here feel formless.
It's a completely different way of life. Back home you wake up in the morning, get on with some shit, go to bed and then do it all again the following day. But anything goes out

here. Outside of scheduled shifts at the club, we're free to do whatever we want.

And besides, doing a shift at the club doesn't feel like work. Certainly not like stacking shelves in a supermarket.

It's all so much fun. It feels like we're at the summer's epicentre. Right in the middle of everything. Making things happen.

Far from reality.

So much has happened to me recently that I'm not even sure where to begin.

Ryan and I have been getting on fine. He's a great guy to live with. Really cool. Laid back. We mostly spend our time together playing PS5 and taking the piss out of the online virgins we usually beat at FIFA. Other times we just smoke weed together and eat junk food. We'll sometimes go to parties hosted by other workers at the club. A lot of them live in our building.

People party after work. People party when they're not at work. People party day and night. It's a constant cycle.

But there hasn't been much in the way of what you might call "serious bonding" between Ryan and me, to be honest. We haven't gotten to know each other in any great detail, but it doesn't matter. Neither of us really cares. The sum total of what I do know is that he's from Edinburgh and supports Hibernian. I don't think he likes to talk much. Those facial tics he suffers from only ever seem to kick in when he's forced into a long conversation or seems nervous about something. So I just leave him alone most of the time. Things are cool as they are. We're totally at ease in each other's company without expecting a lot in the way of meaningful discussions.

Our relationship is what it is, I guess. I can't really say more than that.

Ryan and I work split shifts at the club. One works while the other stays at home.

The Heat of the Summer

We run a tight operation at Pandemonium. We push product on the side. It's a great opportunity to make some extra money. Everyone is in on it.

It's all pretty simple. K-OS distributes a couple of bags to people working their shift. The seller takes a cut. The rest goes to K-OS and Lucio. That's it. No downside. No harm done.

Everybody gets what they want. Everybody goes home happy.

Speaking of K-OS, he seems to have taken a real shine to me. It's a relationship unlike any friendship I've ever had. A real connection. An implicit understanding of each other. He's fun to hang around with and I feel I've learnt so much from him. Not just about the Strip and its goings on, but culturally, too.

He's introduced me to a lot of cool things. Stuff that really challenges me. Makes me see the world from different perspectives.

He loves literature. Art. Opera. These all sit alongside other mainstream interests, like getting fucked up. Hooking up.

He said something to me that really struck a chord. Whatever you turn your mind to at any particular time, it's important to rid yourself of the notion of half-measures. If you party, then you party hard. No excuses. No exceptions.

That was what he offered as an example.

He said it's important that you devote yourself wholly to that interest. That pursuit. That way of life. No compromises. Nothing but absolute intensity. If you get into something, then it needs to become you. Because that's what ultimately makes a person.

You must always crave more than what you already have. More knowledge. More power.

Nobody ever became great through settling.

There's no point living if you're content with your lot, he once told me.

Because you may as well be dead.

The Heat of the Summer

But film is undoubtedly his biggest passion.
We watch a lot of movies together. He likes them graphic. Close to the bone. The more violent the better. He's introduced to me some cool stuff that I never would have encountered otherwise.

He calls this my education.

K-OS will usually put on one of these films while we cut coke together. He projects it on the walls, turns the lights down low for a true cinematic effect allowing the sights and sounds to wash over us.

I find the whole process therapeutic. Something I look forward to. Two friends bonding, shooting the breeze over anything especially taxing.

We talk for hours about everything and nothing while cutting. We even help ourselves to the good stuff on occasion. The pure stuff. A really nice perk of the job. We'll divide a couple of fat lines and hoover them whole as a reward for good work. Then we'll cut the rest with anything that's white and freely available. Flour. Sugar. Salt. Baking soda. Laundry detergent. Soap powder. Anything we can find.

K-OS lives in the penthouse apartment above Pandemonium. The only liveable space in the building. He told me it used to be an apartment block in the years before the island turned itself over to tourism and the families living there were subsequently left with no option other than to leave. The lobby, the basement, the storage units were all demolished in order to create the club.

K-OS mentioned this one night while cutting. He said he took it upon himself to knock through the entire top floor when he first moved in. Not long after Lucio's consortium bought the building. He added that it was a great way to relieve stress. He demolished walls and pillars and posts to leave one giant living space.

He laughed and said that he is Pandemonium, incarnate. That he has been here from the beginning.

The Heat of the Summer

The penthouse is such a model of white-walled minimalism that you can practically hear your thoughts rattle around the open space.

Everything is clear and in plain sight.

The kitchen, the living area, the bedroom, the bathroom are partitioned only by some free-standing Japanese-style paper screens. You can see the silhouette of the person inside moving around. Footsteps echo wherever you go.

Everything inside is functional. From the white leather couch and the small dining table to the glass coffee table we use to cut the coke on.

The penthouse makes for excellent parties. Plenty of space. A great view of the Strip. The music is always loud. Booze and drugs are plentiful. The place is always packed out with Pandemonium workers and others from further afield. All transplants to the island. A cool crowd. Guys who seem to have a lot of money and good-looking girls with tanned skin and toned bodies and long, dirty-blonde hair, with expensive-sounding names like Sapphire and Mercedes and Opal.

Things usually keep going until morning. Sometimes it feels like they don't stop at all.

I asked K-OS one night why he lives at the tail end of the Strip. I asked why here when he could live anywhere on the island.

It was not long after midnight. The music from the bars and clubs several storeys below pulsed along the Strip, seeped into the penthouse through the wide-open balcony doors. The white walls reflected neon shadows.

We were watching a Korean movie called Lady Vengeance at the time. It was a warm, sticky night.

K-OS turned to me with half his face in a red glow. He pushed his sunglasses up the ridge of his nose and smiled.

"You ever read Heart of Darkness, kid?" he asked me.

I shook my head.

"Well, it's a real racist piece of shit. A real motherfucking piece of work," he added. "But there's something I like about it."

"What?"

"It shows the benefits of living amid the madness. Of embracing it. Surrendering to it. It changes you, see. Even without knowing. You get a sense of which way the wind is blowing when other people can't even feel it on their skin. It helps you adapt to your environment. You realise what you have to do in order to get by, you feel me?"

K-OS stopped and returned his attention to the film for a moment.

I remember he shook his head. Smirked.

"It's a fucking jungle out here, kid. Always remember that."

I've been seeing a girl out here, too.

We met at one of K-OS's parties. Her name is Jade. She's from Belfast and slightly older than I am at twenty-one or twenty-two. She's like everyone else in that she's tanned and toned with dirty-blonde hair and a pair of piercing blue eyes. She works the day shift in Pandemonium so we hardly ever cross paths, but I'll often send her a text when I'm heading back to the flat in the early hours of the morning and she'll be there waiting for me and we'll go to bed together and then she'll usually wake first and leave to start her shift.

That's how it works.

We both had the same day off around a fortnight ago. We went for a long walk along the beach, not too far from the spot where the boys and I used to sunbathe. It was just past the summer peak at this point because there were noticeable gaps in the human swell spread across the sand.

We didn't really talk much. We just enjoyed the silence.

I don't think we met up again later that night.

But Jade has helped take my mind off Crystal.

I look back and think how strange that initial infatuation was. I guess the fact that I don't really see much of her outside of work has also lessened that feeling. Even seeing her at work is a rare occurrence. We often work different shifts. And the times we are both in together she is usually up on the surface.

Don't get me wrong, I'm still attracted to her. But I've found she has this cold way about her that is really off-putting. Definitely not a people person. Her comments can often be cutting. She comes across as distant and aloof.

The girls at the club view her as an ice queen. And the guys resent her because she has a direct line to Lucio's ear.

It doesn't help her case that she refuses to socialise with people from work.

I can't recall ever seeing her at one of K-OS's penthouse parties. Or at a party thrown by anyone else, for that matter.

She turns up for work, barely says a word and leaves. Picked up by Lucio in his silver convertible.

She occasionally does some driving for him. A few errands here and there. Stuff to do with supply. When the motorcycle courier is busy. But the general perception among everyone at the club is that she has it pretty easy.

Especially living up in the hills with Lucio. Far from everyone else.

I don't think K-OS likes Crystal that much, contrary to what he has mentioned to me about her being cool or a team player.

I can only guess he says such things to maintain a united front. When he's giving instructions to other members of the team and leans on Crystal's seniority for extra support. I've noticed he's careful not to give anyone so much as an inkling that there could be an issue. He backs up everything she says. Engages her in amiable small talk. That kind of stuff.

But it's a different matter privately. Crystal has sometimes come up in passing during our conversations, but he has been quick to direct our talk elsewhere. Sometimes he has shaken his head at the mention of her name. Become visibly irritated.

I've asked one or two things about her. How long she has been seeing Lucio. Why she never attends any of the penthouse parties. But he has always been reluctant to say too much. His answers have always been vague. Evasive. Deliberately so.

But Crystal no longer occupies my thoughts as much as she used to.

I'm having much too good a time out here to be feeling hung up over her.

16

Hi ... Yeah, Mum ... Yeah, sorry it's been a while. I've been really busy out here. It's hard work. A brilliant experience though. Really worthwhile. I think it will look great on my CV.

Yeah, it's a new number I'm calling you on. It's a work phone ... What? ... Well, I can't use my phone from home out here, can I? The bill would cripple me. That's why work gives everyone a separate phone to use while they're out here. It's only a little crappy thing, to be honest. A bog standard iPhone. Nothing special. But it does the job ... I don't know, I think they must buy them in bulk at a discount because everybody in the club has one.

What's that? ... Yeah, I'll be home before you know it. Don't worry about that ... Mum, you know you'll be sick of me when I'm home eventuall y... No, it was just a joke, Mum. There's nothing to worry about. Honestly.

Yeah, I'd like to tell you about everything, Mum, but I'm not sure I have the time. Life seems to move at a hundred miles an hour out here, but it's weird because I've never felt more relaxed in my whole life ... What? ... Yeah ... Yeah ... Okay ... Yeah ... Look, you know what I mean. It's just the change of scenery doing me good. Of course I'm missing home when you put it like that.

No, Mum, there haven't been any girls. I'm working pretty hard out here. I don't really have the time. It's not the wild ride you probably think it is ... I swear down, I don't have the time ... Yeah ... Yeah, don't worry. I'm still your little boy.

What? ... Oh, yeah, sorry, I forgot to ask about Grandad ... No change? That's good, isn't it? ... Yeah,

The Heat of the Summer

okay. If you say so, Mum ... Yeah ... Yeah, thanks for letting me know. Pass on my love, won't you?

Look, Mum, it's been really nice talking to you, but I have to go. I need to get ready for my shift. They'll dock my pay if I'm late ... Yeah, I know it's been brief, but what can I do? I'm sorry, but it is what it is. I can't do anything about it ... No, I'm not being cheeky, Mum. I'm just telling you how it is ... Yeah, look, sorry. I didn't mean anything by it.

I'm really going to have to go now, Mum ... Yeah, I promise I'll speak more in future. I'll make time ... It's not been deliberate. Honest. As I said, it's just that I've been so busy ... Yeah ... Yeah. But, yeah, we'll talk again soon. Sooner than you know it.

What? ... Home? ... Yeah, I've got a couple of dates in mind, but I'll have to run them by the boss first ... Yeah, don't worry. I'll definitely be home before the end of the summer. Right before I'm due to start uni.

Mum, look, I'm really going to have to go now ... I could talk longer too, but I really can't at the minute ... Yeah, look, I promise I'll call more often in future ... I promise.

Got to go, Mum ... Yeah. Love you too.

Bye.

—

It's another of K-OS's penthouse parties. The place is packed. Everyone is having fun.

A Cardi B song is playing so loud I can barely think. But that doesn't bother me too much. I'm having too much of a good time to care.

I flit around the place. A faint coke buzz in my system.

I'm talking to a lot of different people who have worked at a lot of different places on the island.

The Heat of the Summer

They've all told me not to leave because it will mean I'll have to grow up.

I laugh along with the joke.

I'm trying to keep an eye out for Jade. She is usually at these things, but there's been no sign of her yet. I've tried calling and texting her at different points. Radio silence.

I guess I'll just have to hope she shows. She tends to, anyway.

The worry that I've been a little obsessive pops into my head.

I let myself think it over. I've texted her no more than usual. Rung a few times but hung up when the call went to voicemail.

I think I've been cool. I think I've been okay.

I'm having fun here and that's all that matters.

I snap out of this weird introspection, not allowing myself to get sucked in like I would have done a few weeks ago.

There's a nervous energy in the penthouse. The crowd parts.

Crystal enters the penthouse.

I double-take. Genuine surprise.

It's the first time I've seen her at one of these parties.

I nurse my drink, tracking her around the place. She shifts from group to group making small talk, a wide smile stuck to her face.

It's clear she's alone.

I suspect she knows I'm watching her.

There's nothing I can base it on other than the fact that she has looked in every direction except mine.

Similar to the way I used to ignore Jordan in the hope that it would force him to lose interest in me.

K-OS approaches her. They embrace and smile. Chitchat. A pause.

Then they move in opposite directions without a backward glance.

An arm is draped around my shoulders.

"Hey, kid," K-OS begins, breathing vodka fumes. "Having a good time?"

I gulp back a mouthful of beer. "Yeah. Great party."

K-OS pulls me in close to his chest and keeps me locked in position. He dips his head to stare at me through his sunglasses. "We're tight, kid. Right?"

I nod.

"You feel it? Yeah?"

"Yeah."

"We got a good thing going on. An understanding. We both know each other. We trust each other. Yeah?"

"Yeah," I reply. "I think so."

"Because the shit we do—the cutting and the sorting and shit. The tunes. The movies. The deep conversations. There's a connection there, kid. You feel me?"

"Yeah. I do. Totally"

K-OS breaks the clinch. He fumbles inside his pocket and pulls out a key.

"Give me your hand," he says.

I obey.

K-OS places the key in the centre of my palm, closes my fist and then draws it level with my heart.

"You know what this is, kid?" he asks, thumping my fist against my chest.

"Yeah."

"Trust, kid. It's trust. You guard that thing with your life, alright?"

I nod.

"That thing is a fucking privilege, you hear me? Not

everyone has something like that. It shows how much I value you. How much I respect the work you do for me. *Mi casa, su casa.* You feel me?"

K-OS's pause is swallowed by the background noise of "WAP".

"We do have an understanding, don't we?" he asks, sipping from the tumbler in his free hand.

"Of course."

K-OS nods. "You need anything at all—day or night—you just come round. Let yourself in. You don't even have to call or text. Just come. And I mean that, kid. Cross my fucking heart. You get that? You know that, right?"

"Yeah. Thanks."

He relinquishes my fist, holds me in place with a stony expression.

"Because that's our whole relationship, isn't it kid? We do right by each other, don't we?"

"Yeah."

"And if I ever needed a favour, I could count on you, right? You would do me a solid the same way I've helped you out in the past?"

A firm stare.

"Yeah."

"Good. That's all I needed to know, kid," he responds, grinning.

I look over K-OS's shoulder deep into the human swell, where my eyes lock with Crystal's for the first time all night.

I'm not sure what she's seen. How long she's been watching us.

———

At Pandemonium it's a night like any other. The place is heaving and K-OS is on the decks and the tunes keep

The Heat of the Summer

coming at a frenetic pace. It feels as though the foundations are shaking under the pressure of it all.

Still no sign of Jade. I tried calling her again today. Sent her another text.

Nothing.

I try not to think about it too much. Even if it is more than a little strange.

I try to concentrate on my work instead. Try to stop her from occupying my mind.

It's hard work behind the bar tonight. We're approaching the tail end of summer. The last few blowouts. So I imagine things will continue to be this hectic for a little while longer.

I look out for the motorcycle courier. We're expecting him tonight with the takings from the other parts of the island. It's my turn to take the bag into the back office and fill the safe.

It's a good job we're getting some cash because there haven't been many takers for product recently. Unusually slow business.

No-one can explain why. It doesn't make much sense.

But it's another thing I try not to think about. There's no point worrying about stuff I can't control.

I serve drinks while K-OS burns through his familiar repertoire on the microphone. A cocaine frenzy. He urges the pit to party harder. For longer. The best crowd we've ever had at Pandemonium. The fucking dirtiest crowd we've ever had at Pandemonium. Only the dead sleep. Nothing else matters on this island. Tickets for a boat party, now on sale.

The usual lines I've become accustomed to.

Shrieks rise from the pit, mesh with the opening bars of a Gorgon City song. Strobe lighting blankets the club. K-OS rises on top of the podium and surveys the congested floor below. Bodies surge forward in that same moment. Hands outstretched, reaching out to K-OS.

I sight this picture spanning the entire club over the shoulder of the girl I'm currently serving. I spot a kid who looks to be in his early twenties handing something to another guy of a similar age over by the tunnel. Cash is then slipped to the supplier, concealed in a fist clench.

I scan the place to see if any of my colleagues have noticed this. Everyone else is busy either serving drinks or clearing glasses from tables. The promotions girls keep dishing out vouchers for watered-down fish bowls and shots of dud spirits. Keep hawking boat party tickets.

I take a fifty euro note from the girl I just served and then fire off a WhatsApp message to K-OS as I punch in the code for the till. Let him know what I've seen.

"Got to Keep On" by the Chemical Brothers thunders around Pandemonium.

This is when I notice K-OS check his phone. He studies the screen, the fluorescent glow lighting a steely expression. He nods, sights the crowd and then pockets his phone.

He returns to orchestrating the pit.

I watch the kid move around the club. Weave between bodies. He hands a few more of what I'm almost certain are foil wraps to different people before stuffing the cash he receives inside his shorts pocket. Every exchange is marked with a fist clasp. The kid adjusts the peak of his Nike baseball cap and ventures deeper into the pit.

I become preoccupied. There's a post-2 a.m. lull and it's at this point I'm able to return my attention to the kid, now going about his business with ever-growing confidence.

The sight of Crystal standing in the mouth of the tunnel breaks my concentration. She's plain-clothed, clearly not working a shift. A gym bag is slung over her shoulder.

"What happened to the courier?" I ask her as she steps behind the bar.

But my words are lost in the euphoria of "Castles in the Sky". She doesn't hear me.

Instead I keep my stare trained on her as she makes her way down the narrow corridor towards the back office.

17

It's a penthouse party like any other. Music plays loud. Bright blinking lights are projected onto the walls and ceiling. The crowd ebbs and flows. There are some familiar faces in attendance and others not so familiar. But all of the usual stuff happens regardless.

Yet another amazing party at K-OS's place. Even if it feels as though they're starting to blur into one.

There's a pleasant night-time breeze blowing through one of the open balcony doors. The temperature has dropped noticeably in the past couple of days. It's much cooler of a night now. I'm finding it easier to sleep.

Crystal is again in attendance. She's been showing her face at more of these things recently.

I've no idea why. The other thing I've noticed is that there's been a distinct change in her demeanour. More open. Approachable. A lot friendlier.

Again, I can't explain why.

K-OS zips around the room. High-energy. Flying between different groups. Talking rapid-fire and laughing loudly.

He spoke to me earlier about needing to step up production. Increase distribution. Maybe even cut bigger quantities with the usual shit.

He said all this wide-eyed, coming over intense. His forehead almost pressed to mine.

Overbearing to the point where I just wanted him to leave me alone.

He's been a little off tonight. I've been around him plenty of times before when he's hoovered up fat lines of uncut powder, but he's never behaved like this before. Never been this hyped.

And again Jade isn't here. Still AWOL. Still no

response to my calls and my messages.

But I'm trying not to give her too much thought. Like I always say.

I feel let down by how things have turned out, being totally honest. She could have told me straight up if she had suddenly decided she wasn't interested in me.

But I don't suppose it's anything worth getting too worked up about. Stuff just tends to happen out here. No point allowing yourself to get bogged down in every little detail.

It's some time past midnight and I'm a little drunk and I've found myself talking to Crystal.

It's a largely inconsequential conversation. Basic pleasantries. And I don't mean that disparagingly. It's the kind of low-key chat that I'm grateful for right now. Nothing too heavy. All perfectly amiable.

It's a nice contrast to how she usually is.

I think Crystal is pissed too, but a few drinks behind me. I can't tell if she's on anything else.

A wide smile is etched across her face, laughter lines running parallel to her mouth. Her eyes are wide and full, giving prominence to the faint outlines of crow's feet.

"I've noticed you and K-OS have been getting on like a house on fire," she says.

"Yeah. He's a good guy. Really fun to be around."

"What do you do when you hang out?"

"Watch movies. Listen to music. Stuff like that. Nothing too far out of the ordinary."

"A little bird told me you have a key to this place."

"Yeah, that's right."

She looks impressed. "I'd consider that an honour. K-OS must really think a lot of you to do that."

"I guess so."

I expect her to follow up, but nothing comes. She instead stirs her drink and continues smiling. A conspicuous silence.

It's one of those strange situations when a conversation has run its course but neither person has an idea of how to bring it to a close.

I let out a yawn and excuse myself. Crystal giggles. I tell her it's been a long day.

"Can I ask you something?" I eventually say.

"Yeah?"

"You know Jade?"

She crinkles her brow. "Who?"

"You know the girl I was seeing for a little while?"

She shakes her head.

"From Belfast," I say. "Tanned, dirty-blonde hair."

She smirks. "Sounds like you've just described me there, Luke. Apart from the Irish part, obviously."

"Yeah, I guess," I reply, letting out an uncomfortable laugh. "She usually works the afternoon to early evening shift. Or at least used to. I haven't heard from her in ages. So I was just wondering, really."

Crystal shrugs. "There are tons of people at the club that I have no idea about. It's a pretty big operation. It's hard to keep track of people, given the high turnover. She probably just went home, Luke. It's really shitty that she didn't get in touch, but I don't think it's anything to worry about."

"Yeah," I say quietly, staring into space.

We sip our drinks at the same time.

"How come Lucio doesn't come to these things?" I ask. "Out of curiosity."

"Not really his scene, babe." She pauses, lifts the tumbler to her lips to take a swallow. "And besides, he's away at the minute. Business trip."

The Heat of the Summer

The shatter of glass interrupts our conversation. Not the noise of a bottle smashing as it hits the ground or a mirror accidentally being broken, but the ear-splitting sound of a whole pane splintering into a million pieces. A noise which immediately attracts everyone's attention regardless of how fucked up they are, prompting a sea of heads to turn in the same direction. Screams and surprised gasps fill the air.

It comes from the balcony. There's a guy on the ground, rolling from side-to-side on a bed of broken glass. His face is cut and bloodied.

K-OS breaks from the gathered crowd, storms over to the guy and drags him to his feet by his shirt collar, hurls him against the stone balcony wall.

Everyone moves towards the balcony. Jostles for a better look of what's happening.

The crowd in front of me is half a dozen deep but I'm able to see the guy crawling on his hands and knees, glass shards crunching under his body weight. He coughs and spits blood.

K-OS slow-steps, stalks the guy. He reaches down to clamp a hand around the throat. His free hand then seizes the hem of the shirt to lift him up, forcing him back against the balcony wall.

The guy's face is a picture of terror. K-OS raises him even higher, tilts him backwards, half over the edge. The guy screams, wails apologies. Repeatedly gargles the word "sorry".

I file through to the front of the crowd. Nobody seems to possess the inclination to intervene, content instead to rubberneck.

The guy has pissed himself. A dark stain over the crotch of his sky-blue shorts. His legs kick the air.

K-OS's face is pressed a half-inch from the guy's.

The Heat of the Summer

"You fucking leave. You fucking leave right now, you hear me?" K-OS barks. "This is my fucking house. My fucking turf. You think you can fuck about with the biggest dog in this fucking yard? You fucking think again, you little piece of shit."

The guy mumbles something.

The noise from the Strip momentarily pierces the commotion.

Cheers. Jarring laughter. Dance beats. Distant sirens.

"You leave. And you leave now. You understand?" K-OS threatens in a slower, more controlled voice. "And if I ever see you or any of your friends around here, I'll fucking kill you all. I'll fucking slit your throat like a fucking calf. You hear me? You fucking hear me? And don't think I won't. I fucking dare you, son. Just you fucking try me."

K-OS snaps back and releases the guy to send him sprawling at the feet of the crowd. No-one stoops to help the guy, who is now wheezing and struggling for breath. He plants his palms against the glass-scattered balcony floor for support. A thin trickle of bile seeps from his mouth.

K-OS steps behind the guy and grabs him by the hair, yanks back his head to elicit a loud snap. K-OS then looks into the guy's eyes, chuckles. "I'd cut your throat right now, boy. But I want you to tell your friends about this. Tell them everything I've just said to you. You repeat every word to Teardrop. You understand, son?"

The guy nods. His whole body trembles.

K-OS shoves the guy's head into the glass. The guy rolls into the foetal position and convulses, clutching his midriff.

The exact spot where K-OS aims a hard kick.

K-OS then moves back through the crowd.

"Party's over," he calls out, heading towards the kitchen area. "Somebody get that piece of shit out of my fucking flat before I do something that will make this ten times worse."

The crowd disperses. Some shuffle out of the apartment. Others grab their belongings.

Two kids from Pandemonium lift the beaten mess of a guy to his feet.

I'm rooted to the spot here. Unsure of whether I should approach K-OS or leave as instructed. I look over to see him at his kitchen worktop filling a tumbler of ice with whiskey. He draws the glass to his lips and takes a huge gulp.

I cast my eyes around the emptying apartment a second time.

Crystal has already left.

18

K-OS and I cut in silence.
The wind blows into the penthouse through the open balcony doors. The noise from the Strip is a background buzz.
It's been getting marginally quieter, marginally cooler each night.
There's no movie playing on the walls tonight. K-OS said the projector is broken.
We cut and cut and cut. Our knives scrape and squeak across the glass-topped coffee table.
K-OS hoovers up more of the good stuff than he would normally. He cuts. Leans forward. Bows his head. Snorts. Not a word said.
He takes his knife and cuts some more.
I just get on with the job. I don't take any tonight. I'm not feeling it.
K-OS is in a black mood. It's just the two of us in the penthouse tonight.
He has probably only grunted two whole words to me. Both were to acknowledge my presence after I let myself into the flat.
I've not wanted to look at him tonight. In case he accuses me of staring too hard. Or acting weird, or something.
I don't really want to do anything which could cause him to suddenly flip.
I let him stew in whatever ill feeling is affecting him.
And so we cut and cut and cut in complete silence.

—

I text Jade.
The message fails to send.
I call Jade.

The line cuts dead.

———

Pandemonium shuts at stupid o'clock in the morning and I finish my shift by tidying the pit. I sweep up broken glass and all kinds of lost belongings. Earrings. Wallets and purses. A pair of ripped lace knickers. Mop the sticky residue staining the floor. Spilt drinks and dried blood.

I do this on my own.

A lot of my colleagues have been distant lately. Meagre conversation. Very little personal interaction.

I think they have noticed how close K-OS and I have become. I think word's got around that I have a key to the penthouse. And I can only assume that it's made a lot of people jealous.

But I try not to let it bother me. I try my hardest not to think about it.

And speaking of K-OS, it was a relief to discover he wasn't DJing tonight. You tend to lose track of the days out here, so remembering things like what night someone is due to work can often be an issue.

I felt pent up approaching the club earlier. Just thinking about being in the vicinity of K-OS again.

It was a tension which lifted when Crystal told me it was his night off.

I relaxed immediately. Caught my breath.

It's odd to think a friend is having this kind of effect on me.

I normally take the lift up to K-OS's penthouse at the end of my shift. Even on nights he isn't working. Simply to hang out. Maybe watch a film or split a bag while he puts on some music. Or just to listen to him talk.

But I don't feel like it tonight. It's the last thing I

The Heat of the Summer

want to do. I'm sure he will be expecting me, but I plan on heading straight home tonight. Avoid his darkening mood for one night at least.

I zone out thinking over all of this, mopping the same bit for several minutes, when Crystal approaches.

"Hi, Luke."

"Hi," I respond, snapping out of my trance.

"Shift okay?"

"Yeah. Not too bad, thanks."

"You really start to notice the drop in footfall towards the end of the summer, huh?"

I nod. "Yeah."

"You going up to the penthouse tonight?"

"Sorry?"

"K-OS's place."

I shake my head. "No. Not tonight."

"How come?"

"I don't know," I say. "I'm a little tired, to be honest. I think I'm just going to go straight to bed."

"Do you want a lift?"

"What?"

"Do you want a lift?" Crystal repeats. "The car's parked around the back. I don't mind dropping you off."

I pause. "No, it's okay," I say, drenching the mop. "I don't want to put you out. I don't mind getting the bus."

"You sure?"

"Yeah. But thanks anyway."

She flashes a kind smile walking back towards the tunnel. Says she'll see me tomorrow.

My colleagues dotted around the club all stare at me.

They've all heard the boss's girlfriend engage me in friendly conversation and offer me a lift home.

As usual, I try to keep my worries from forming. I concentrate on cleaning an area I've already cleaned spotless.

———

I arrive home totally wiped. There's no sign of Ryan in the front room, which is weird because he can usually be found playing *FIFA* and smoking a joint whenever I return home, regardless of the time of day.

The birds outside have started singing. Anaemic sunlight passes into my bedroom through the thin curtains drawn across the dirty window.

"Living the life of a vampire," I remember Ryan commented when I first told him my shift patterns.

I take a shower.

It's not something I usually do after finishing work. But I feel like I really need one right now.

The hot water cascades over my body. I relax, shut my eyes. My head empties of all my worries one by one.

I return to my room. Check my phone.

A missed call from K-OS. A text from K-OS.

No show tonight? The fuck is that about?

I put my phone on silent and climb into bed, gaze wide-eyed at the ceiling.

"Kernkraft 400" by Zombie Nation beats through the walls, grows louder with every passing minute.

———

Ruby's death was the catalyst for my parents' divorce. They had been having issues for a while, but I guess they were manageable. A few heated rows that were quickly forgotten. One would vent at the other and then a period of terse silence would follow and some kind of normality would eventually resettle. I'm not suggesting that it was an especially healthy way of managing their relationship, but it worked for them for the most part. For many years, in fact.

But Ruby's death magnified everything. It brought all of their problems to the fore with such intensity that they could no longer be ignored. There was no escape, no reprieve from the situation they found themselves in.

Maybe things would have been different if Ruby had survived. I'm aware how trite that sounds, but it's something I can't help but think from time to time. I wonder if they'd have muddled along, or worked out their differences in their entirety. Maybe they would have split up regardless, and I'm just overthinking all of this.

I honestly don't know.

Mum and Dad began to drift apart not long after the funeral. Mum was a mess, as you would expect. She sometimes flat-out refused to get out of bed. And the times when she managed to, she couldn't bring herself to see anyone. She would just drift from the bedroom without changing from her pyjamas or doing anything to her appearance and would slump on the couch for hours at a time, gawping into space. Sometimes she would take herself into the kitchen, where she would stare out of the window above the sink with a view of the garden.

Dad was also in pieces. But he managed to keep it together during the day. He maintained a stoic demeanour and tried to keep some routine. He took some time off work to look after Mum and I can recall he put on a brave face to me by saying it would mean we would be able to play football together and watch a lot of TV, but this never transpired. All of his time was spent keeping an eye on Mum and ensuring the house was tidy.

I would approach him to see if he wanted to do something fun and he responded each time by saying that we would later through a thin, weak smile that I could see through even as a kid.

But it would be a completely different story of a night.

That was when Dad would crash.

He would tuck me in at night and wish me sweet dreams. Leave a kiss on my forehead. But I would be unable to sleep no matter how hard I forced it. I would close my eyes and hope that the tiredness would do the rest, but my mind refused to switch off. I would end up spending hours gazing up at the bedroom ceiling.

That was when I would hear Dad crying.

It was the only time he could be truly alone with his thoughts. There was no longer anything to distract him after Mum's needs had been met and the household chores had been taken care of.

The television would blare through the house until way past midnight in the days and weeks after Ruby's death. I would hear Dad's wailing come from downstairs over the persistent crackle. Footsteps from the living room to the kitchen and then back the other way. The empty beer bottles I would find resting beside the couch in the morning an indicator of how many times he had taken that trip during the night.

I wasn't allowed to go to Ruby's funeral. My parents said I was too young. They thought it would be too upsetting for me. I suspect they were right, given that I remember they both looked worn-out when they picked me up afterwards. Both of them had red eyes.

I spent the day with Grandad instead. He was understandably pretty subdued. I can imagine he was upset at having to miss his granddaughter's funeral, but I think he realised at the same time that it was the only option.

The Heat of the Summer

He did his best to keep me occupied. We watched a lot of television that day, I remember. That in itself was a rarity when visiting my grandfather because he was normally quite active. We would play out in the garden, or I would help him out in the garage that he converted into a woodwork shop when he took early retirement. We would sometimes go to the park or the beach for a long walk, depending on the weather. There was nothing of the sort on that day, though. We just spent hours on the couch allowing the colours of the television to wash over us in a daze.

I think I watched *The Wizard of Oz* for the first time that afternoon. Grandad noticed that it was on and couldn't believe that I hadn't seen it. Or if I had previously, I had no recollection of having done so. He promised me that I would love it.

And he was right. We watched in complete silence. I think he was grateful for the respite it provided. I was entranced by everything I saw on screen. Everything from the colours to the characters, the contrast between Kansas and Oz struck a chord. It left a lasting impression in a way I could barely conceive back then.

I've obviously had to keep this quiet for the past few years because it would do nothing for a teenager's street cred, but it remains my all-time favourite film to this day. I don't know if it's the film itself or the memory of watching it on such a sad day which has influenced my choice.

But there was always something that puzzled me about the film, even watching it back then. I could never understand why Dorothy was so keen to return home. Kansas was bleak. Kansas held nothing but unhappiness and boredom. She had friends in Oz. She had adventures in a strange and interesting land. She was someone important. Somebody who was cherished. Not just some anonymous farm girl, expected to do whatever her aunt and uncle thought best.

The notion of escape revealed itself to me that day. The fresh promise and limitless potential that escape inspired.

I remember thinking that I would love to be able to get away from everything.

—

My phone bleeps.

A text from an unsaved number. One I don't recognise.

Leave me alone. Stop contacting me. It's for the best.

19

K-OS and I cut in silence.

Soap powder and bicarbonate of soda tonight. Ever-increasing amounts.

A movie plays on the high white walls in front of us. I've forgotten the title, even though K-OS has twice told me what it's called.

I don't want to ask him again.

It's an Italian film from the early 1980s. That's about all I can remember from the introductory speech that K-OS gave while fiddling around with his brand new projector.

The film is about an American film crew shooting a documentary on Amazonian tribespeople. I watch grainy footage of an amputation. Animals are mutilated. Someone is impaled. There's a gang rape. A forced abortion. A beheading. All of this happens as my eyes flit back and forth between the wall and the coke stacked on the table.

"Handheld 16mm cameras," remarks K-OS. "Fucking beautiful, kid. Makes it look more real than life itself."

I watch the unfolding action with a neutral expression. Try to mask my unease.

K-OS points at the pictures with the knife he is using to cut the coke. "This film, kid," he starts, "do you have any idea about the kind of shit it caused when it was released?"

I shake my head.

K-OS smiles. "All kinds. The animals being killed—that shit is real. And some French magazine suggested this was a snuff film. That the human killings in it were legit. It was so convincing that a murder rap was added to the director's obscenity charge. Fucked up, huh?"

I say nothing.

"Funny thing is that the actors who died in the film had to sign contracts that they couldn't appear in shit for one whole year after the film's release," K-OS continues. "That strengthened the case against that fucked-up Italian cat. The whole thing looked real. These people were nowhere to be seen. What's that old saying, kid? If it fucking talks like a duck and walks like a duck... Know what I'm saying?"

He pauses for a moment. Snorts.

Scenes from the film are reflected in the lenses of his sunglasses as he faces me. Colours coat his cheeks.

"It was only when the director showed the fucking court all of these pictures of the actress hanging out with the crew after the shoot that the charges were dropped." K-OS stops and laughs. "How fucking insane is that, kid? You shoot something so realistic that everyone believes it actually happened. I fucking love that. Fucking with people to that extent."

He lets out another hard laugh.

"And that's what I love about this movie, see. It hits that exact sweet spot between reality and art that everyone has been trying to replicate since. Real-life brutality captured through an other-worldly lens. And you know what, it makes you think about absolutely fucking everything. And I mean fucking everything, kid. It really fucking displaces you, when you consider how thin that line between reality and art actually is when you watch something like this. And that makes you wonder about your own perspective on things. Whether you can see that line and can make a clear distinction, or you're just going with the flow and happy to embrace the mayhem because it's all one and the same. Whether you figure that everything is so messed up that there's just no point trying to disentangle it all. So you let it all slide and just think to hell with it. You know what I'm saying?"

A silence falls. Background screams.

"So how many times have you seen this film?" I ask him.

"Too many to count, kid," he replies, shaking his head, still beaming.

—

There's been no sign of Ryan for a couple of days now. I'm a little worried, being totally honest.

Not that I've mentioned any of that to K-OS or Crystal. I'm not sure how it would go down with either. I don't know if Crystal would consider it any of her concern, seeing as they more or less work different shifts. Maybe she would view it as out of her remit. And she's already made it clear that a high turnover of staff is natural out here.

Everyone is dispensable, she stressed. It's no great loss if someone suddenly decides to skip their shifts.

As for K-OS, there's no telling how he would react. I'm not even sure if he knows that Jade has gone missing, come to think of it. These are not the sort of things I've spoken to him about.

The point is I don't really want to find out. I don't want to give him an opportunity to lose his temper.

I would be more relaxed if there was a clear indication that Ryan had simply decided to go home. And that's the main issue, in fact. There is no sign that he packed his things and left. He seems to have just left, full stop. His PS5 is still connected to the TV in the living room. His toiletries still clutter the bathroom.

The Heat of the Summer

Framed photographs of who I presume are his family, and other assorted knick-knacks like miniature *Star Wars* figurines, are dotted around the place.

It's as though he's disappeared.

I went into his bedroom out of curiosity. The wardrobe was full, as was the chest of drawers. His bedside cabinet was packed with Rizla papers and condom wrappers and crisp packets.

There was no evidence to show that he had booked a flight home.

My apprehension grows each time I come home to an empty flat. One that's still full of another person's belongings. This racks my brain whenever I take a shower, eat breakfast, even when I sit on the couch and try to numb myself with endless games of *FIFA*.

I try to stop it, but it's almost impossible.

The quiet in the flat reminds me of the silence I associated with the big house in the weeks and months after Ruby's death. An intimidating, pronounced silence that endured even under attempts to drown it out with noise.

The house looked exactly as Mum and Dad had planned it to at that point, some years after moving in. Each room conformed to their design. I was pleased with how my bedroom looked. I loved the living room. But it was impossible to shake the sadness that cloaked the house.

Mum did her own thing. She would help me get ready for school and pick me up and cook my tea, but it was done dispassionately. Not once did she break into a smile or a grin, or allow a note of laughter to leave her.

She was my mum, but not my mum at the same time. I know that sounds confusing, but it's the only way I can describe how she was. Far away from the person I

The Heat of the Summer

knew and loved.

Dad was largely absent, meanwhile. That became his way of coping. He was a workaholic anyway, but Ruby's death took that to a whole new level. He would even sleep at the office on occasion.

But Mum had stopped questioning his habits. She just left him to it. And beyond that initial period of care, Dad similarly left my mother to her own devices.

It was a strange period typified by that blanketing silence.

I wasn't capable of forming such thoughts at the time, but it strikes me now that we were essentially three different people living under the one roof. The family connection that bound us had all but disintegrated. The only thing we shared was a surname.

I can't recall how I processed this. If I was even able to at all.

I knew that I was sad. I knew that Mum and Dad were sad.

But I think I knew subconsciously that there was a lot more to it than simple sadness. The emotion that I'd only known previously when I lost a football game or was grounded. Even back then, it seemed ridiculous that what my parents and I were feeling could be cured by something as banal as ice cream, or half an hour watching TV. The usual stuff that always chased away the sadness.

I wasn't sure how this would play out. Whether it would ever be possible for this sadness to leave us. Whether we would end up carrying it around forever.

I remember thinking—one Saturday morning when Mum refused to get out of bed and Dad had already left for the office and I was left to eat cereal in the living room as cartoon after cartoon washed over me, barely registering—whether things would ever get better.

It's something I find myself thinking about now.

—

The TV news out here is playing a story of what I guess is a dinghy full of people drowning at sea. I've barely picked up a word of the language because there has been no need to.

I watch the television and try to piece things together from the pictures.

The police and medics and forensic teams are gathered on a beach I don't recognise. I presume it's the mainland. Members of each unit amble to and fro, as though every action is a cursory effort for the cameras. There's a punctured dinghy cordoned by some metal forks draped with torn police tape. Bodies are covered with white sheets and spread five or six feet apart from each other across the sand.

One last call to the unknown, unsaved number I received the warning text from elicits only a dead tone.

There are a lot less people working at Pandemonium.

20

It's a night like any other at the club. The crowds are thinning but the atmosphere is the same as at the height of summer. K-OS goes through his routine on the decks. Crystal patrols outside. A motorcycle courier comes in at some point and hands over a gym bag to a colleague, who takes it through to the back office.

It's a good job the numbers are dying off because me and the five or six others working inside the club ordinarily wouldn't have been able to keep up. Things are still busy, but it's at least manageable.

There are more and more people pushing product down in the pit. It was just the one kid at first. But now he's being joined by a half-dozen others. They're more brazen about their business. The concealed handshakes have become open exchanges. Nods and hand gestures, increasingly expressive. Money flagrantly pocketed.

It's the subject of quiet conversation among staff. We're making less and less each night. After the shift, our pockets remain stuffed with unsold wraps of cut product.

It's after closing time.

My colleagues made a half-hearted effort at tidying up, clearly eager to leave. They've left me to deal with most of the shit.

K-OS has already departed. He descended from the podium, head bowed, eschewing eye contact and conversation as he stormed through the tunnel towards the service lift up to the penthouse.

I'm all alone in the club. The blazing lights expose the mess of broken glass and discarded plastic cups all over the pit. Waste and debris amid a sea of lukewarm alcohol flecked with vomit and blood.

The Heat of the Summer

I stuff some rubbish into bin liners, stack the dishwasher and then give the floor a barely-bothered mop.

The rest of it can wait until morning. I'm far too tired right now.

I make my way up the tunnel, my footsteps the only noise, and head towards the entrance bathed in the ghostly light of very early morning.

Crystal is hanging around, pacing outside the entrance while tapping her phone. She looks up as I approach and gives a friendly smile.

"Just waiting to lock up," she says.

I nod in response and give her a hand closing the cast-iron double doors. We talk amicably, walking through the archway bearing the club's name to step out onto the deathly quiet Strip, where the neon blink has been shut off.

Burnt-orange sunshine rises above the charcoal buildings around us. A warm breeze blows down the cobbled street.

We stand still, facing each other awkwardly.

"Let me give you a lift home," Crystal says after a few seconds' silence. "And I won't take no for an answer this time."

The morning bus is hell. It's always packed with people returning home after their shift. Not just workers from Pandemonium but staff from the other clubs the length of the Strip. The body heat is excruciating. It's impossible to settle. There's barely a chance of getting a seat so you're normally pressed tight up against somebody while grabbing a handrail.

I always feel like a zombie after my shift. I suppose that goes for everyone else. All I want to do is collapse into bed. Even if you're fortunate enough to get a seat,

The Heat of the Summer

it's still a real effort to switch off and unwind. Because there is always something that brings you back. Reminds you where you are. The vehicle's suspension aching over bumpy roads. The suffocating air.

So I decide to take Crystal up on her offer this time. Especially seeing as there is no-one around to pass judgement or—even worse—spread a rumour.

The top of the silver convertible is down but the air conditioning still blows cool on our faces. I'm able to breathe easy, stretch my legs. I melt into the comfortable leather seat and rest my arm over the side.

"Push the Feeling On" by Nightcrawlers is playing on Spotify. A slower tempo to the version usually played in the club.

"You like the car?" Crystal asks.

"Yeah," I reply. "Lucio's?"

Crystal nods.

"How long have you been with him?"

She purses her lips and pauses, screws her face in thought. "A few years now. Hard to say exactly. The years tend to merge out here. Time seems to move at a different pace. All this time spent on this island and I've never been able to understand how or why."

"Yeah. I know what you mean."

The drive takes us from the concrete heart of the island out towards the amber flatlands. A mountain range dominates the horizon. Skeletal high-rises on either side of the road we're driving along stretch into the distance.

The scenery changes gradually. We're approaching the residential swell mostly housing nightclub workers. There is a supermarket on one side. A Burger King on the other. A petrol station. A garage. A small, dingy bar.

"So how long have you been out here, then?" I ask

Crystal.

She keeps her eyes on the road ahead. A row of uniform concrete buildings opens out in front of us. The purr of the car's engine and the low-playing stereo are the only noises aside from the occasional snippet of birdsong.

"Since I was eighteen," Crystal replies coolly. "Came out here on holiday. Enjoyed it so much that I decided I didn't want to leave." She turns her head towards me as we stop at a set of traffic lights stuck on red. "You know how it goes, don't you, Luke? Isn't that exactly what you did?"

"I guess so." I stop for a moment as the lights change. "So how old are you now?"

She flashes a benign smile. Mock-scolds. "Didn't you know it's rude to ask a lady her age?"

"Sorry, Crystal," I mumble, embarrassed.

"Don't call me that outside of work."

"What?"

"I said don't call me that outside of work," she repeats. "It's not my name."

"What's your real name, then? Or is that out of bounds, along with the age thing?"

"It's Alice," she says. "And there's no need to be a smart-arse, mister."

"So Crystal is…"

"Strictly a work thing. Alice is a bit old-fashioned, don't you think? Makes you think of some middle-aged frump. And, by the same coincidence, it's also my mother's name. So I've got her to thank for that one. But, anyway, who would you rather buy boat party tickets from? Crystal or Alice? Who would do a better job of enticing you into the club? Who would you rather have make eyes at you?"

"I think Alice is quite a nice name."

"Well, it's been a long time since anyone has called me by it. Certainly out here. Probably not since the friends I came out here with went home."

"Not Lucio?"

She shakes her head, shrugs her shoulders. "I'm basically whoever he wants me to be. He thinks I play the part of the dutiful girlfriend quite nicely."

Another stop at a set of traffic lights.

Alice continues, sighing. "I try my best to keep things separate. Personal from professional. Try to keep a clear distinction between the two. But it's difficult, you know? One inevitably takes over the other the longer you're out here."

A brief silence. The music plays low.

"How come you didn't go to K-OS's place after work?" Alice asks me.

"I'm trying to keep my distance, to be honest," I reply. "I'm worried that I'm being seen as a bit of a teacher's pet by everyone at the club."

"It's not the only reason, is it?"

"What do you mean?"

"His temper, for a start," she says. "The mood swings. They're something else, aren't they?"

"Yeah. I think I'm best just leaving him alone, to be honest. Let him cool down for a little bit."

"You don't have to justify yourself to me. I've known the guy for a long time now. I know what he can be like."

"How come you two don't get on?"

"Is it that obvious?"

"I don't know," I respond slowly. "I'm not sure if the other people at the club have really noticed it. But it's something I've picked up on. A weird vibe. I've got a

The Heat of the Summer

sense of it from hanging out with K-OS. I've noticed how uneasily you two interact a lot of the time. And you don't really go to the penthouse parties much."

Alice shrugs. "You've got to do what's best for business. You don't have to like your colleagues, do you? As long as your feelings don't impact your working life, I don't suppose there's any real issue. Like I said before, Luke, I try to keep a clear distinction between personal and professional."

"So is that why you don't get on? His personality? Are you two just like oil and water?"

She purses her lips. "One of the reasons. There are far too many to mention. I'd probably end up getting bummed out if I listed them all. But there's a history there. A lot of complex shit."

"Right."

"And, frankly, I wouldn't really feel comfortable talking about the guy to someone who is pretty close with him, present hiccup aside obviously." She stops for a few seconds. "No offence," she then adds, smiling.

"None taken."

"I mean, you two do have a special relationship, don't you?" she asks. "You still have a key to his place, after all?"

"Yeah," I confirm, conscious of the keys weighing heavy in my pocket all of a sudden.

She slows the convertible to a stop at the junction that precedes the hard right leading to my building. She applies the handbrake and turns in her seat to glance at me side on.

"Look, Luke," she begins. "I don't know how you'd feel about this, but Lucio is still out of town on business. Would you like to come back to the house for a drink?"

21

The journey to Alice and Lucio's place takes us along a coastal road. We're so far away from the dense concrete pockets clogging the island that we may as well be in a different world. The transformation I'm witnessing emphasises the weirdness of the island's geography. Its bewildering layout. I'm still to get a sense of my bearings even after being out here for a couple of weeks.

The sea is shimmering over to my right. The sun is rising. Morning is breaking and the colour of the sky is receding to a tranquil blue.

It reminds me of that first hour I spent out here all that time ago, when the coach took us along those rickety hill roads from the airport and I was able to see all of this for the first time.

A memory that feels surreal after everything that has happened since.

I angle my head towards Alice, whose eyes are fixed ahead at the road winding alongside the shore.

"Can I ask you something?"

She sighs, clacks her tongue against the roof of her mouth. "Sure."

"Do you know Ryan has gone missing?"

"Your room-mate?"

"Yeah."

"And you're worried?"

"A little bit."

"Why?"

"Well, people don't just vanish into thin air, do they?" I say. "People—especially people you live with—usually tell you if they're going somewhere, if they're moving out. It just seems a little weird to leave without saying a word. And I've tried to call him but there's been no answer. I'm a bit worried, to be honest."

"I wouldn't if I was you."

"Why?"

The Heat of the Summer

"People come and go all the time," Alice answers. "The work is pretty casual. It's pretty common for people to suddenly up sticks and leave. For a lot of reasons. Whether they're tired of the work or they have commitments back home. Trust me, Luke, it happens all the time."

"Yeah. You've told me that before."

"So why are you worried, then?"

"Because all of his stuff is still in the flat."

Alice remains focused on the road, offering only a slight shoulder shrug. "As I said, it's not something I would be majorly concerned about. He may have just decided to leave on a whim. This line of work doesn't often attract the most stable and centred of people, in case you hadn't noticed. A lot of people tend to do as they please. Like that girl you were pretty close with. What was her name again?"

"Jade."

"Right, right. I remember now. But the point I'm trying to make, Luke, is that people are disposable out here. It's something everyone involved is conscious of. If someone decides to leave, finding someone to replace them is no great hardship. Lucio likens it to fishing," she says. "You catch one and it can be a keeper. You catch another and you might throw it back, or just accept it if it wriggles off the hook. It's just how it is out here. I wouldn't beat yourself up worrying too much."

"But she left without saying anything to me. That's what I don't get. She didn't reply to any of my calls or messages. It was as if one day things were fine, and then the next she just decided to forget everything and fuck off."

"I don't know what to tell you, Luke, and I don't mean to sound cruel, but that's exactly what I imagine happened. I sympathise, but as I said, people come and go without a word exchanged and it's accepted. It's just how things are out here. No-one like that is a great loss. We know and they know what they're getting involved with. It's an unwritten contract. Casual work in exchange for a good summer. If people decide to quit on us, then we just go with it. I know it can be

The Heat of the Summer

tough when you get attached to someone but there's nothing more I can add, really. She probably got what she wanted—a few weeks of partying without a care and a cheap, meaningless fuck... No offence."

I turn my head, stare at the sea. The stretch of blue that's a constant reminder of how far I am from home.

"Right, right," I reply in a quiet voice, distracted by the soft roll of a wave. I then look back at Alice. "I get what you mean, but why haven't these people been replaced? Have you noticed how there are fewer and fewer people working in the club each night?"

"The summer is coming to an end," Alice shrugs. "It's what happens. It's a revolving door of people from the spring onwards. Not many stick around when the temperature drops. And it's no real concern because business drops at the same time. It's all pretty manageable."

"I guess... But there's something else I've noticed."

"What?"

"Dealers in the club," I say. "A lot of people I don't recognise, pushing product. People who don't work at Pandemonium. Plain clothes."

Alice shrugs again. "You'll have to take that up with K-OS, I guess. But you've not spoken to him in a while, have you? Maybe it's the kind of thing you two would talk about while cutting. Maybe neither of you has had a chance to bring it up."

"I don't know."

Alice snorts and then shakes her head. "What do you want me to tell you, Luke? That the club is being invaded and we're on the cusp of some fucking gang war?"

She pauses, plays with the stereo's volume.

"Look, it's K-OS's operation," she continues in a more measured tone. "It starts and ends with him. He pushes the product on the premises with Lucio's consent, a cut is taken and everyone is happy. Lucio just leaves him to it. I'm sure K-OS has everything under control. What is it they call it when a business offers new services, new products?

Diversification? Maybe K-OS has taken the load off you guys so you can just concentrate on selling fish bowls and shit. I don't personally like the guy, but I at least recognise that he's pretty good with this kind of stuff."

I look straight ahead. "Yeah. I suppose."

"You're not a natural-born worrier, are you, Luke?" Alice smiles, turning to face me. She then throws back her head giggling. "You need to let all of this go, and relax. I want to split a bottle of wine with you and chill, not act as if I'm your shrink."

Alice puts on a pair of Wayfarers and we turn off the coastal road and drive inland through an upper-class residential area composed of identikit white stucco houses with orange clay-tiled roofs. Tropical flowers are in full bloom. Palm trees line both sides of the road. The scent of freshly-cut grass laced with lavender and rose hangs in the air.

There are signs that the place is stirring to life. Curtains twitch. A garage door opens. A paperboy riding a battered old bike becomes visible in the convertible's wing mirror. A gardener's van pulls up to a kerb.

The car climbs a steep gradient. The stucco houses are spaced further apart up the lush green hill, typically confined by wrought-iron gates and high white stone walls wrapped in ivy. The gaps in the gateways offer glimpses of luxury cars and swimming pools and sprawling lawns.

The grounds exude calm.

We arrive at one such house at the top of the hill. Alice stops beside a security box fixed to a stand and punches in a code to open the iron gates. She guides the convertible over a paved driveway and inside a red-brick garage detached from the house, where she parks next to a collection of sports cars.

Alice leads me out to the front of the stucco house. It's noticeably bigger than those we passed along the way. A slight chill in the air prickles my skin as we step beneath the sloping canopy crowning the entrance.

"The house that Pandemonium built," Alice remarks, opening the front door.

The interior is immaculate white from floor to ceiling the whole length of the vast hallway. A marble floor. A row of silver-framed rectangular mirrors fixed to the walls. Twisted chrome stands holding vases and glass ornaments and empty crystal candelabras. Diamond-cut ceiling lights. The strong smell of bleach.

A draught blows through the house from the open living room door. Soft piano music comes from upstairs. The thud of footsteps through the ceiling. I instinctively glance upwards, attempt to locate the source of the noise while following Alice into the living area.

It's open-plan. Another expanse of brilliant white. The walls reflect the early-morning sunlight streaming into the room through the open balcony doors, the thin white curtains flapping with the breeze. There are a couple of cream sofas and chaise lounge sofas all positioned around a frosted-glass coffee table in front of an LCD TV above a blocked fireplace. Blotted canvas prints resembling Rorschach tests decorate the walls. There are a couple of bookshelves over in the far corner near the balcony doors.

Alice heads over to a kitchen station to the right of the living room entrance and plucks a bottle from a wire wine rack without looking. "I love an early-morning glass of wine," she sings. "Night-shift workers of the world unite."

She notices that my attention is directed beyond the balcony, down at the rolling garden comprised of trim grass and manicured rose bushes and embankments leading down towards a teardrop-shaped pond flanked by water features. The amber hills lie far beyond the stone walls surrounding the grounds. The old town, far below. A thin strip of sea visible in the distance over to my right.

"Take a better look if you want," she says.

I step out onto the balcony and grip the railings. The warm sun laps my face. I use the flat of my hand to shield my eyes from the rays, squinting at the same time.

The Heat of the Summer

"It's a gorgeous view," Alice pipes from inside the living room.

"Yeah," I call back to her, nodding.

I go back inside the living area.

More noise comes from upstairs. Footsteps pacing across the floor.

"Are you sure there's nobody else here?" I ask Alice.

She shakes her head. "Maybe the cleaner," she then adds. "She has her own key. Usually lets herself in."

"Can you hear that?"

"Luke, will you come over here and sit down and stop stressing? Have a nice glass of wine to take the edge off. I presume you like white?"

She is relaxed on the couch with her legs bent and her feet tucked up to her side. One arm is propped against the armrest, her head resting in her open palm. Her other arm is folded across the back of the couch. Two filled glasses of white wine rest on stone coasters on the frosted glass table.

I sit down next to her. She stretches forward to hand me a glass, which I take.

"So do you enjoy working at Pandemonium?"

I take a mouthful of the wine.

It tastes funny. Disgusting, even. A lumpy, coarse texture. A chalky under-taste.

I watch Alice talk out of the corner of my eye, her words disintegrating into a monotone drone. Her lips move, but I fail to comprehend whatever she's talking about. She smiles and gesticulates, and I can only guess that the bob of my head encourages her to keep speaking. I blink and everything becomes distorted like looking through a cracked lens.

A pounding at my temples announces itself. An ache in my brain.

Tiredness takes hold.

The last thing I'm aware of is the sloppy smile across my face, seeing Alice through a murky haze as the colours around me fade.

—

The Heat of the Summer

Dead air.
Darkness.
Out of which a picture of Mum and Dad emerges.

They're both shouting at each other across the dining table. Mum is on her feet. She is angry and in tears. Dad is sat down, ashen-faced and motionless. He stares straight ahead. He keeps saying he's sorry.

My parents are to divorce. Dad has announced that he's leaving. He has met someone. Someone from work. A young intern. Early twenties. He tells Mum that he never meant for it to happen. It just happened.

Mum throws a plate against the wall behind him. Dad barely flinches as it sails past him and smashes to pieces. She howls something indecipherable. She asks him how he could do such a thing. Repeatedly.

Dad says he's been suffering.

Mum says she has been as well.

Dad replies that he has needed somebody to talk to. He's needed support.

Mum answers that she has always been here. She's barely left the house.

Dad shakes his head and says he doesn't mean like that. He adds that she hasn't been right in the head for a long time.

Mum screams. Pulls her hair. She turns around and punches the wall. She yelps and shakes the pain from her cracked knuckles.

Dad looks, embarrassed, at the dining room floor.

Mum collapses over the table. She sobs. Her chest heaves. Her arms are spread across the table and she pulls them in closer to her body and buries her face in her bent elbows.

Dad gets up. The metal chair legs scrape against the floor. He walks around to the opposite side of the table and tries to smooth Mum's hair. She bats him away without looking up and continues to wail hysterically.

Dad stares at her wearing an uncomfortable expression. His bottom lip trembles for a moment. He looks straight ahead at the dining room door. He walks over, wraps his fist around the handle. He then glances back, adjusts his eyes to the ceiling so as not to make it obvious that he's taking one final look at her.

The door closes.

Mum's crying rings through the dining room in the big house, continues to echo as the picture dissolves.

I wasn't present for this fight. But I just watched it all unfold out of the impenetrable black as though spying through a keyhole.

A clear picture in my mind's eye.

I heard an abridged version of what happened from Mum. She still made reference to that "slut of an intern", though. Still mentioned that Dad had left us to shack up with a child.

I never heard Dad's side of the story. I've barely seen him since he left. There's been no contact at all for the past three or four years.

I got the impression that I was an inconvenience to his new life. A reminder of what he left behind.

So one day I took the decision to stop seeing him. He didn't seem to take issue with it.

Not that I explicitly told him about this. I just stopped responding to his texts and his calls. I can only assume that he wasn't too bothered about it. He never sought me out personally. We simply stopped corresponding. And that was that.

It was as if there was no relationship there to begin with.

22

Daylight seeps through my eyelids as I come around. My eyes flicker. I take a few deep breaths before opening them fully.

I feel groggy.

Everything is as blurry as when I first passed out. It takes a few seconds for the fuzz to clear. For my vision to sharpen.

The distortion crystallizes into coherent shapes. A chaise lounge. A TV. A frosted-glass coffee table. It takes a moment for me to realise where I am, never mind remember what happened. The sun licks my face, paints everything in starker focus.

I realise that I'm bare-chested. My Pandemonium T-shirt is draped over the back of the couch. The contents of my pockets have been emptied onto the coffee table. Keys. Phone. Loose change.

"Good afternoon," I hear Alice call from behind me as I shuffle upright on the sofa.

My face burns red. I scramble for my T-shirt and put it back on. I open my mouth, let out a groan.

"Hi."

"Feeling rough?" Alice asks. She sets a cup of coffee on the table in front of me next to my things and sits down on the chaise lounge.

She's wearing a white silk dressing gown. Her hair is scrunched up in a messy bun.

I rub my forehead and then run my hands back through my hair. "What happened?"

"Turns out you're a bit of a lightweight," she smiles.

"What do you mean?"

"A couple of mouthfuls of wine and you were done. You've been out for a solid couple of hours."

"I don't remember a thing," I reply.

"Well, maybe that's for the best." She nods at the cup of coffee. "Drink that. It'll sort you out."

I reach for it and take a sip. My neck creaks angling my head towards Alice, who has pulled out her phone from her dressing gown pocket. "This might sound ridiculous," I begin in a strained voice. "But..." She looks up from the screen. "...Did anything happen between us?"

She smiles. Laughs. "Don't be ridiculous, Luke. That's not why you think I invited you back, is it? I just thought a little company might be nice. It can get really lonely here at times. Especially when Lucio is away."

I screw up my face. "No, no, I was just checking, that's all."

"Yeah. Okay."

"I'm so sorry about last night. I must have just taken the knock. Too many late nights catching up with me."

"Well, I think you're off tonight, if I've checked the rota correctly," she says without looking up from the screen.

Silence.

Alice glances at me over her phone. A hint of concern registers on her face. "Finish that coffee and I'll call you a taxi. I'll raid Lucio's stash and give you the money for the journey home. It'll be quite an expensive trip." She pauses and looks me up and down, furrowing her brow. "Get some rest tonight, Luke. Promise me? You really look like you could do with a quiet night in."

―

"Ruby Tuesday" plays on the radio in the taxi cab.

I'm cold. Run down.

I press the button for the window beside me to shut.

I ask the driver to change the channel as best I can.

I slow my speech. Enunciate every syllable. Even gesture with a twisting motion.

Typical dickhead semaphore that I'm still forced to call upon when talking to locals.

The driver turns the radio up louder.

I slump back in the passenger seat and watch the world drift by outside.

The Heat of the Summer

The lift opens in front of me and I make my way down the dingy apartment block corridor.

I'm in a total funk. Not a hangover but a feeling of lethargy. Completely drained and disoriented.

The coldness from the car journey has followed me. My teeth chatter. I cross my arms across my chest and keep them tucked in tight as the lights around me dim.

I arrive outside the flat, take a mouthful of stale air and fumble in my pocket for my keys.

It's only on pulling them out that I see that the door is six inches ajar. The hopeful thought that Ryan is back flashes through my mind. But this is quickly extinguished upon noticing that the wooden frame is splintered, the front door slightly cracked.

The lights are on. The place has been trashed. My clothes and other belongings have been strewn all over the kitchen and living area.

A clatter comes from my bedroom.

I move quietly into the kitchen. My hand shakes, opening one of the kitchen drawers, and I wrap my fingers around the handle of an unwashed butcher knife.

The noise comes through louder.

I creep towards the bedroom. I lift the knife level with my shoulder. I shift around the wedged-open door, peek inside. The room is dark apart from my bedside lamp, which emits just enough light for me to make out a figure near the wardrobe.

I force the door wider and yell. I slash through thin air and throw myself on top of the intruder to send them hurtling backwards onto the bed. I clamber onto their chest, pin them to the mattress.

I draw back the knife. Our screams combine.

The guy I'm on top of looks to be in his early twenties. He's wearing a pair of horn-rimmed glasses and has his light-brown hair shaved at the sides, with a gelled fringe.

"What the fuck?" he screams repeatedly. "What the fuck? What the fuck?"

I wrap my hand around his neck. I notice that I've accidentally cut his arm in the confusion. Blood seeps from the open wound and onto the bed.

"Who the fuck are you?" he says, choked.

"Me? Me? Never mind that shit. Who the fuck are you? And what the fuck are you doing in my bedroom?"

"Your bedroom? What the fuck are you talking about? This is my fucking bedroom. My fucking flat."

"No," I respond, shaking my head while lowering the blade a couple of inches towards his face. "No."

"Where's Ryan?" he rasps.

"What? How do you know Ryan?"

"Because this is my flat. He's my room-mate."

"No, I'm Ryan's room-mate."

"Do you work at the club?" he asks.

"What club?"

"Pandemonium."

"Yeah."

"So do I."

"No you fucking don't. I've never seen you work a shift there before."

"Because I've been away," says the guy. "How long have you worked there? A month or so?"

"Something like that."

"Well, that explains it then," he answers, growing calmer despite the blade hovering over him. "I was sent away before you started work."

"Sent away? What do you mean, 'sent away'?"

"Abroad. Sourcing."

"What?"

The guy rolls his eyes, sighs. "Look, how about you do me a favour and get off me, okay? I can't explain everything with you sitting on top of me, can I?"

I stay still.

"Let me prove I'm telling the truth," he says. "I promise I won't do anything. I won't attack you. I swear. I need to mop up this blood and sort myself out as well."

The Heat of the Summer

I remove my hand from the guy's neck. Climb off him. I let him get to his feet but keep the knife drawn by my side. He spots this. "Don't be silly, mate. Just put the fucking knife down, okay? I'm not going to suddenly pull out a pocket knife and start cutting you up. It's not fucking inner-city London."

I do as he says and set the knife down on the bedside table.

"Good," the guy says. "Now give me a second to clean myself up and we can get to the bottom of this."

23

The guy returns from the bedroom after five minutes carrying a large towel under his arm. He has a damp hand towel tied around the cut on his arm.

He throws me the large towel.

"Just put that over the blood stains," he tells me. "If you're anything like me, trips to the launderette are a rare occurrence."

I spread the towel over the dried marks on the bed sheet.

I took a look around my bedroom while he was in the bathroom. All of my clothes have been removed from the wardrobe. Most of my things have been thrown out of the room. There's an overturned chest of drawers taking up a lot of the floor space. A suitcase is propped up in the corner of the room.

"Goes without saying that I'm sorry about the forced entry. Gone for fucking two minutes and they decide to change the locks. Unbelievable. The paranoia surrounding this place is off the fucking scale," he mutters. He then pauses, makes eye contact. "I'm Kevin, by the way."

"Luke."

Kevin dips his hand into his pocket to pull out his phone. He sits down on the edge of the bed. He taps at his phone and addresses me without looking up. "Now, Luke, first things first—some proof that I'm not bullshitting you."

The phone itself is all the proof I need. The same five-year-old iPhone as mine. The same model every Pandemonium worker has.

He turns the phone towards me and thumbs through a few photographs. Pictures of him at the club wearing a Pandemonium uniform. Pictures from parties at K-OS's penthouse. A selfie with K-OS. Pissed selfies with Ryan, his gold tooth catching my eye. Pictures taken in this very flat. In this very room.

"See?" he says as he pockets the phone.

"I don't get this," I answer. "If what you're saying is true—"

"Which it is."

"If what you're saying is true," I repeat, "about this being your flat, then why would they move me in here?"

"Who took you up here?"

"Alice."

A blank stare.

"Sorry, I mean Crystal."

His eyes roll to the ceiling. "Oh, her," he snorts. "Lucio's fucking Rottweiler. One cold customer, that girl. I swear she only got with Lucio to avoid the trips abroad. Fucking devious bitch."

"But why would they move me in here?" I ask again.

Kevin shrugs. "Maybe they thought I wasn't coming back."

"What are you talking about? I don't get this."

His lips form a half-smile. He points to the suitcase in the corner. "Do me a favour, just grab that for me. Open it up."

I grab the case, lay it flat and unzip it. Crumpled, dirty clothes spill out over the sides.

Kevin shakes his head. He reaches for the knife on the bedside table and stretches across the floor to hand it to me. "No," he says. "I mean really open it up."

"What?"

"The lining," he explains. "Cut the lining."

I take the knife and make an incision in the black fabric lining. I cut straight along, then down the narrow edge of the case. The lining folds over to reveal a stash of thick brown envelopes. Roughly half a dozen.

"Go on. Take a look," Kevin says.

I take one of the envelopes. I rip the top and reach inside and pull out a block of cocaine tightly wrapped in Clingfilm.

"Shit."

"How did you think we got hold of the stuff?" Kevin asks.

"I don't know. I never really gave it much thought."

The Heat of the Summer

"Did you think it just grew on trees out here?" I drop the package on top of his clothes. "Well, no, obviously not, but..." Silence. I'm lost for words. "I don't know," I concede.

"Everyone at the club has a job to do, mate."

"Meaning what?"

"What I said before," Kevin says. "Sourcing."

I look at him confused.

He sighs. "It's like a rite of passage. Everyone working at the club has to go to South America at some point and bring back a ton of this shit. No ifs. No buts. No excuses. It's the law. There's a rota and everybody's time comes eventually... Well, except for Crystal, as I mentioned. Sucking Lucio's shrivelled dick obviously excludes her."

"So I'll be expected to go over at some point?"

"Yep," Kevin nods. "It comes to everyone sooner or later, like I said."

I run my hands back through my hair and then hide my face.

Kevin continues. "And I'm not going to lie, mate. It's tough. It's really fucking tough. And it's only gone and become a hell of a lot harder recently. Make no mistake, I'm fully aware of how lucky I am. Some people end up in prison, you see. Some don't even make it back at all."

I angle my head towards Kevin and pinch the corners of my ears to prevent tears from forming. "Do you think that's where Ryan is? On a drugs run?"

"No. No way," he says, shaking his head. "I definitely would have heard about it if he was. Lucio controls our movement on that score. K-OS makes the arrangements, communicates them to Lucio, and then he gives the green light. Nobody can go anywhere without the say-so of either of those guys."

"What do you mean?"

"Ryan isn't the first to disappear," he explains. "People get an inkling that they might be next and make a run for it. But as I said, seeing as Lucio controls our movement, it usually involves transportation which you wouldn't really call safe or even reliable. Literally taking your life in your hands."

"This doesn't make a lot of sense," I reply. "When you talk about Lucio controlling our movement, what do you mean?"

"Okay, let me put it this way—when they moved you in here? Where did you put your passport?"

"In the top drawer of my bedside cabinet."

"And you're sure it's still there?"

I open the top drawer and sift through a heap of crap. Coins. Batteries. My phone charger. Takeaway menus. All of it gets tossed to the floor as my search turns frantic. I end up sliding the drawer out from the cabinet and tipping out the contents before throwing the thing across the floor in frustration.

I collapse onto the bed. Stare hard at the ceiling.

"He takes everyone's passport, mate. Obviously to keep everyone grounded. He only gives someone their passport back when their name comes up on the rota," Kevin says. "You see, the embassy is on the mainland, so the only way home is to make a break for there. But seeing as K-OS has contacts who work the ferries, it's easier said than done. The only other option is the most dangerous. Taking a chance in some shitty little fishing trawler if you can convince someone to take you. Or pile inside a fucking dinghy or something. You're at the mercy of the waves because we're talking miles of choppy waters beyond the beaches."

"And you think that's what Ryan has done?"

Kevin shrugs. "Possibly. I don't suppose there's any way of knowing."

"Why didn't you make a run for it" I ask, "before they sent you to South America?"

He shrugs a second time and takes a lighter and a pack of cigarettes from his pocket. He sparks up. Takes a long, deep drag. "You're taking a huge chance whatever you do. It's not

The Heat of the Summer

as if one is completely without risks. You may as well flip a coin."

I open my mouth but no sound comes out.

"It's probably best not to think about Ryan now. If he's safe and sound, the thought of it will only bum you out. If he's not, then..." His voice trails in between tokes. Another shrug. "I don't know. It's not really worth thinking about either. It's why you're best not making too many friends out here. People come and go. They're dispensable, mate. Wait—disposable, even. Maybe that fits better. Regardless, we're all just fucking commodities on this island. No hiding from it, man."

The room fills with smoke during a long and uncomfortable silence. I haven't moved from the bed, still looking up at the ceiling. Kevin is sat on the floor with his back propped against the wardrobe. He's gazing into space, his only movement the occasional lift of his right hand to raise the cigarette to his lips.

I roll over onto my side.

"So what happens?" I ask, eyeing Kevin.

"What do you mean?" he asks, puffing smoke.

"The drug runs to South America. What happens?"

"Well, first of all, K-OS gives you the flight details and drives you to the airport and—"

"Spare me the fucking sarcasm," I interrupt. "I'm a fucking wreck here. There's no need."

He holds up a hand. "Sorry," he responds through a faint smile. He pauses to flick ash into an empty Coke can lying amid all the crap on the floor. "K-OS gives you a contact. Someone Lucio knows. You pick up the stuff, you pack it, and then you hope that the dogs at the airport have blocked noses or something."

"Jesus."

Kevin nods. "It's fucking scary, man. And as I'm sure you can imagine, they're not nice people. You just want to get in and out."

"How many people have been arrested?"

"It's hard to say exactly. We don't keep official records of this kind of thing. But I'd say maybe there's a one in three chance of making it back here safe. One in three chance of getting arrested. One in three chance of getting killed. Spin the wheel and take your pick."

I shake my head. Rub my temples. Push some vomit back down my throat.

"There's a war going on out there," Kevin goes on. "A fucking guerrilla war. You're constantly having to watch your back. It's as if there's a target on you from the minute you step off the plane. It's exhausting, mate."

"Fuck."

Kevin stubs out the cigarette on the rim of the Coke can. He flips the butt into an overturned waste paper bin. "I don't really know the ins and outs of it, to be honest with you. But I think some guys out there are putting the squeeze on Lucio's boys. I don't know if they've muscled in on someone else's turf or whatever, but things have gotten really bad. Thinking logically, I guess Lucio and K-OS thought I wasn't coming back and that's why they gave you my room. Each trip out there is taking longer and longer."

"I think something similar is happening out here," I respond. "A war."

Kevin nods. "It is. It's getting there. What was that period before World War Two called when there was no fighting for a long time after war was declared? The Phoney War, was it?"

"I don't know."

"Well, that's where we're at now," he says. "We're building up to something."

"Yeah."

"It's been on the cards for a long time," Kevin continues. "K-OS gets high on his own supply. Cardinal sin. He's tried to expand the operation to compensate for the money he puts up his nose. And obviously you stand on other people's toes by doing that. There's this guy—Teardrop—who K-OS has majorly pissed off. He runs a similar operation on the other side of the island and has a market share on the mainland. There's always been an uneasy peace between the two. Both stick to their own patch and that's that. But obviously K-OS has reneged on that recently to ensure that Lucio isn't out of pocket. And you'd better believe that a stunt like that comes with its own consequences."

"Like this Teardrop guy sending his own people to push product in the club?"

"I'd say that's the first strike. A warning shot, maybe." Kevin clenches his lips. Pauses. "But mark my words, Luke, things are only going to get worse. And pretty quickly, too."

24

I'm on the couch tonight. Kevin won best of five at rock-scissors-paper for the bedroom.

All of my stuff is out here now anyway. I'll probably start moving it into Ryan's room tomorrow.

I've pretty much accepted he's not coming back. Same with Jade.

I lie wide awake thinking all of this over.

—

A hard nudge to the shoulder forces me from my sleep.

I let out a moan. Stir.

My eyes are still shut but I'm conscious of somebody trying to wake me. Somebody staring at me.

I roll over onto my side in the hope that this is a dream.

A second hard nudge. A couple of slaps to the cheek.

A familiar voice penetrates the darkness. "Wake up, kid."

I open my eyes to see K-OS hunched over me.

The sight of him without sunglasses catches me by surprise. So much so that I almost let out a cry at what they've been hiding all this time.

His right eye stares at me lifelessly. A glass prosthetic. A long crescent scar curves around the outside of the eye. Bright white half-moon stitches.

K-OS smiles wide, watching me wake up.

"K-OS," I splutter. "What are you doing here?"

He pats my shoulder, growls. "You're going to pop your cherry tonight, kid."

"What do you mean?"

"You'll see," he murmurs, tipping his head towards the wide-open front door. "Get dressed, kid. You're coming with me. You don't get a say in this."

The pallid ceiling light covers K-OS's face. He looks bedraggled, as though aged horribly in the days I've been avoiding him. Deep lines have formed across his cheeks and around his lips. His beard is unkempt and overgrown, with prominent grey patches. His head hasn't been shaved either,

The Heat of the Summer

hair allowed to grow without thought. Silver streaks pepper the thin black fuzz tapering to a widow's peak.

"Where are we going, K?"

"Remember what I said about nothing coming for free out here?"

"Yeah."

"Well, now it's time to pay your debt, kid."

We head outside.

The wind howls. Freezing cold. The summer drawing to a close.

K-OS's white Chevrolet is parked at the kerb. He instructs me to get inside. I do as he says without a word.

I strap myself into the passenger seat. K-OS turns his keys in the ignition. The engine snarls and we drive off into the dark, past the other apartment blocks.

The roads are empty.

We speed through the concrete swell and emerge out the other end as K-OS thumbs through a playlist to soundtrack the drive through the flatlands.

The opening bars to "Hotel California" play through the speakers. K-OS taps the steering wheel and nods his head in time with the music. He keeps his focus firmly ahead through the windshield at the bumpy road illuminated only by the shallow white pool of the car headlights.

I ask him where we are going.

No response. Only the music fills the silence. His stare remains fixed into the distance.

K-OS's mouth opens in time with the song. He speaks the words under his breath.

Certain lyrics are more audible than others. I hear him mention about not being able to kill the beast. About checking out but never leaving.

The car slows climbing a steep hill. The roads become narrow and winding. The vehicle's suspension jerks. The engine screeches.

K-OS's expression remains unmoved.

The Heat of the Summer

I shift in my seat, turn my head and stare out of the window at the darkness. I can still make out the faint outline of the sea. Completely still. Tinged with moonlight.

No end in sight. No sign of the horizon.

I look at K-OS. "So where are we going, K?"

No reply.

I remain still. Try not to let it show that I'm scared.

I mirror K-OS's expression. Keep focused on the dark road ahead.

The car veers off-road. The terrain feels harder. More treacherous. Stones crunch. There are sudden jolts and shudders. I grip my seat belt to keep myself in place.

The headlights point at a small stone shack with a corrugated-iron roof and a large metal door. The windows are boarded up. The surrounding landscape appears bleak and barren.

K-OS kills the engine.

The wind strikes the car windows.

And still K-OS says nothing. He looks straight ahead at the stone shack. He shuts off the headlights, causing the shack to sink into blackness.

It comes as a surprise when K-OS speaks. He doesn't turn his head to face me, maintaining the same gaze out of the window.

"Open the glove compartment," he orders.

"What are we doing here, K?"

No answer. The wind cries outside.

I pop open the glove compartment.

"Take it," K-OS says.

I reach inside, feel something hard and metallic. I clasp my hand around the object.

The shape and its weight are a giveaway.

My voice cracks. "K?"

"Take it," he repeats. "There are some gloves in there as well. Put them on. Take it. Wipe the thing."

"K, what's going on?"

The Heat of the Summer

He twists his head to the side, fixes me with a scowl. He throws out a hand and hits me hard across the back of the head. He does this a few more times as I throw up my arms to protect myself. But each strike finds a way through my defence. I instantly feel dazed and I bite my bottom lip to stop it from trembling, force back the tears.

"Did I fucking lose my nerve?" he seethes quietly. "Did I hesitate? Did I fucking equivocate, you little shit? Did I not make my instructions clear enough?"

"What?"

More hard strikes to the head.

Tears pour down my face. I angle my body awkwardly so he can't get a direct hit. I press my forehead against the window. My palms are outstretched, pleading for mercy. I keep murmuring "please".

"Now you have finished critiquing my communication skills, I would like you to fucking do as I asked," he says. "Put on the gloves. Take out the gun. Wipe the thing."

I keep my head bowed, my eyes fixed on the floor as I take out the gloves and put them on, my whole body shaking. I then grab the handgun and wipe the handle using the sleeve of my hoodie.

"Let's go," K-OS says, opening the car door.

"K, what are we doing here?"

It's a question I regret asking the second it leaves my mouth. I tense in anticipation of another beating.

But K-OS only grins this time. He keeps a hand clasped around the doorframe and arches forward so that his face is inches from mine. A single dry chuckle leaves his throat.

"I told you, kid, we're going to break you in," he answers. "Gently. The way all considerate lovers should."

K-OS uses the torch app on his phone to light a path to the shack. I follow behind, holding the gun tight with both hands.

The metal door has been wedged open using a broken breeze block and some snapped timber. K-OS grips the edge and forces the door open wider. The rusting metal hinges emit a long, jarring creak.

We step inside. The stench of stale piss burns my nostrils. I hear the squeak and scurry of rats. K-OS throws the light around the dilapidated shack to reveal bales of hay stacked against the back wall and rotting wooden beams extending from floor to ceiling. There are pigeons gathered in the rafters, the wooden frames caked with bird shit. K-OS keeps moving the phone around the place, seemingly frustrated at not being able to find whatever it is he wants to show me.

The light eventually settles on a kid. He's about my age. Pale. Gaunt. Clearly scared. His brown eyes bulge in the harsh beam. Surprise registers before settling into a look of horror. The kid's hair is messy. There's dirt and cuts and scrapes all over his face. He's tied to a chair with his arms forced back behind the plastic frame. A strip of duct tape covers his mouth. There's a dark, wet stain around the kid's crotch.

"K, what's going on?" I ask, turning to him.

K-OS doesn't respond, still eyeballing the kid hard. He then offers his phone to me and spits something about making sure I keep the kid lit up.

All I can manage is a feeble "okay". I shift the gun into my left hand and take the phone with my right, ensuring the beam is focused on the kid the whole time.

The kid squints at the light, tries to tilt his head away from the glare, only for his chin to sink into his chest.

K-OS approaches the kid. He pulls a knife from his pocket.

The kid's whimper is audible through the duct tape until it's ripped from his face. He looks at K-OS, lifting his head from his chest, breathing heavily. The duct tape has left a vivid claret mark across his mouth.

K-OS glances at me over his shoulder. "You filming this?"

I fail to respond.

The Heat of the Summer

"Are you filming this?" he repeats in a firmer tone. "I want this on film, kid. I want every little detail captured."

I nod. "Yeah. Uh-huh," I say as my thumb skips across the screen to the record function.

"Good. Because, Mr DeMille, I'm ready for my close-up."

After delivering the line he plunges the blade deep into the kid's chest. There's a piercing cry spliced with K-OS's chuckling. He steps around the kid and slashes at will. Each incision prompts more laughter from him.

The kid's screams subside with each cut.

A low gurgle. Blood seeps from his mouth. He coughs up bile. The kid's head sags from one side to the other.

My hand shakes, capturing this on film. I watch it all unfold through the screen.

K-OS carves the kid's cheek. He steps around the chair, dips his head. He extends his free hand and holds the kid's face in his palm. He presses the kid's forehead against his stomach, tries to calm the mewling with a long shush. K-OS then turns the hand in which he carries the blade and runs his knuckles down the side of the kid's face.

"Don't worry. It will all be over soon. Not too much longer," K-OS says, breaking into a slow, mumbled rendition of the chorus to "Three Little Birds". He cuts the singing abruptly to shoot me a serious look. "You've definitely got this on film, kid?"

"Yeah," I respond.

"Good. Because it's time a message was sent loud and clear. This is our home. Nobody fucks with us. There's no fucking Geneva Convention-style shit afforded to POWs in this conflict."

K-OS clasps his fingers around the kid's chin, jerks his head to one side. He lowers the blade to slice off a portion of the kid's lobe. The lump of flesh drops to the floor in a puddle of blood.

The Heat of the Summer

K-OS crouches down, picks up the lobe and pockets it along with the blade. He sends a wide grin straight down the lens.

"Souvenir," he remarks. "I always make sure I get one. I'm a sucker for the gift shop."

The time between the kid's faint breaths grows longer.

K-OS steps towards me, filling the screen.

"Shut that off now," he orders, making a cutting gesture with his blood-stained right hand. "You're up, kid. Time to finish this thing."

K-OS takes his phone from me and props it against a rock so that the kid is caught in the light. He extends an arm and wraps it around my shoulder, pulls me in close.

"I'll help you through this," K-OS soothes, his lips pressed to my ear. "I told you I'd break you in gently."

K-OS guides me towards the kid, whose features are all the more horrific up close. Blood streams from the wounds scoring his face. His clothes are soaked. The kid gapes at me open-mouthed, the colour in his eyes diminishing.

I look beyond him, far into the surrounding blackness.

K-OS whispers in my ear. "You've got this, kid. I promise you. You've got this. I've laid the groundwork. Now you just have to finish the job. There's no going back now, kid. This is it."

He locks his hands around mine. I raise the gun under his guidance. He pushes my palms forward, positions the gun so that it is dead level with the kid's mouth.

"Open wide, fucker," K-OS snarls, relinquishing a hand for a moment to pinch the kid's nose.

The kid's mouth opens. K-OS forces the barrel of the gun inside.

The click of the kid's teeth clamping down on metal goes through me.

K-OS feels me shiver. He whispers for me to relax. "Let's take it slow, kid. I want you to remember your first time. Let's make it special."

The Heat of the Summer

I catch a glance from the kid. His eyelids droop. His face has turned grey. He starts gnawing at the gun in his mouth.

K-OS's voice travels through the darkness. "I'll count you in, kid. Okay?"

I must have nodded without realising because K-OS begins his count.

"One…"

He locks his fingers around mine.

"…Two…"

He guides my fingers around the trigger.

"…Three."

There's an explosion. A ringing in my ears.

The force throws me backwards into K-OS, who stops me from falling.

The gun throbs in my hand. An intense heat. I drop it to the ground with a clank.

My eyes remain closed. I let out a cry.

I press my face into K-OS's chest and feel his jacket become damp with my tears.

He wraps a hand around the back of my head and begins patting my hair, shushing after each stroke.

He tells me that it's over.

—

We leave the shack.

Day is breaking. Streaks of burnt orange puncture the black sky.

I ask K-OS what we're going to do about the body.

"It's Lucio's patch," he says, shrugging. "All of this will be apartment buildings in six months, anyway."

25

Early morning.

A picture of serenity forms over the sea. A clear blue sky. The sun climbing ever higher above the horizon.

I glance absently out of the car window. From this vantage point high up in these dusty mountains, I see what I'm certain is the agricultural village I spotted on that coach ride from the airport so long ago.

That song from Midnight Cowboy—"Everybody's Talkin'", I think it's called—is playing in the car.

K-OS hasn't stopped talking since pulling away from the stone shack. I tune in and out, distracted by nothing in particular out of the window.

He talks about power. True power. Exactly what it is. He offers examples and shares his logic. He says that true power is only doing something once so that everyone sings from the same hymn sheet. He says that true power is being both feared and respected simultaneously. He says that true power is people knowing their boundaries before the question even enters their heads. He says that true power is having the rule of law bend to your will.

—

Hi, Mum ... Yeah, sorry it's been a long time. I've been really busy ... No, I haven't been avoiding you, I swear. I've just forgotten to call you back, that's all. Honestly, it's nothing sinister. It's shift work, Mum. Mostly night shifts. That's why. I'm basically sleeping all day and working all night. So it's hard to find a time that's suitable ... Yeah, I know I could have texted, but— ... What? What? Sorry, Mum ... Yeah, I know it's no excuse. I'm sorry.

But, yeah, it's been an experience. I feel like I've learned a lot. About myself and life in general ... Yeah ... Yeah ... Yeah, it's been tough, but fulfilling.

What, Mum? Coming home? Soon ... Yeah, very soon, Mum. I'll have to have a word with my boss to sort out the

exact dates, but it will be soon. And you'll be the first to know.
Grandad? He's taken another turn? ... Oh, that's a shame. I'm really sad to hear that. He can't catch a break, can he? ... Well, that's good at least. At least he's in good spirits. He's always been good at putting a brave face on things, hasn't he? He's always been a fighter ... Yeah, I promise that the first thing I'm going to do when I get home is go round and see him. Grab some cakes. Have a cup of tea.
Look, Mum, I'm really sorry to cut this short. I've got a lot of stuff to do at the club and the line is really bad ... No, honestly, I'm fine. I'm absolutely fine ... I think you're just being paranoid there, Mum. I'm just a bit tired, that's all.
Yeah, Mum. I'll see you later. I promise I'll keep in touch.
I love you too ... Bye. Bye.

———

There's a party going on. Somewhere in the building. It's loud and it's boisterous, the clatter of footsteps pounding the floorboards and the harsh reverberation of unrestrained laughter. The echoes of distant dance beats ripple the air.
I'm trying to sleep. But I can't.
I pull my pillow over my ears. The noise still seeps through.
The conversation between Kevin and some girl he has picked up comes through the thin walls all muffled and unclear. Her laughter grates. Eventually the distortion firms into groaning and grunting, the repeated strikes of a headboard against plasterboard. Mattress springs squeak.
I roll over. I wipe the sweat from my brow and pull the soaked sheets tighter around me.

———

K-OS and I cut in silence.
He's put on some opera. Something by a guy called Philip Glass. It's about the pharaoh who introduced Egypt to monotheistic religion. That's according to K-OS, anyway.

The Heat of the Summer

That's about all he has said to me the whole time. I don't feel like asking him any questions.

The strings and vocals play over our cutting. Bicarbonate of soda. Soap powder. Sugar. It all goes together indiscriminately. Then neatly packaged into wraps and bags.

You have to take pride in your work, he's told me so many times before.

We haven't spoken about that night. I have no urge to raise the issue.

Another night at the penthouse.

K-OS is perched on the couch. He would fall to the floor in a heap if he shuffled forward even an inch. He glowers at the film on the walls and occasionally breaks from his introspection and lowers his head to the coffee table and snorts a line of the pure stuff before resettling into position.

Grainy images flicker across the walls. Disturbing images. Half-clothed women having their throats slit. Naked men being castrated. Violent angry orgies. People being whipped and strangled with spiked leather belts. Young girls with flat tits and bald cunts who look to be on the cusp of puberty having blunt objects stuffed inside them. A boy who looks no older than eighteen tied to a meat hook in a slaughterhouse, gutted from sternum to stomach.

The pictures themselves are largely distorted, shot out of focus, blurring into each other. The chilling screams accompanying the images are the clearest part of the movie.

I don't ask K-OS about the scenes. What film they're from. If this is a montage featuring several scenes cut together. If it's an arthouse or avant-garde picture, or whatever pretentious title you want to give. I don't even want to broach the possibility that they're real.

And that's why K-OS and I cut in silence tonight.

26

It's a bright, beautiful day. Typically warm, though noticeably cooler than during the summer peak.

I'm sat outside a café in the old town nursing a coffee. There's an old couple deep in conversation at a nearby table. A young family at another. Some teenagers giggling in earshot. Locals move listlessly around me in different directions.

The day is drifting by with a languid, carefree pace to events.

I say that, but still feel tense. I'd like to think it's the caffeine in my system, but I haven't felt right in a long time. I haven't slept properly in days. My sunglasses mask the bags that may as well have been forged beneath my eyes. But any passer-by would probably consider me to be in good health based on the light tan of my skin.

I feel incongruous in my surroundings despite appearing completely at ease. The indecipherable chatter of a language I've made no attempt at learning surrounds me. The tuneless plink of stringed muzak piped through the speakers attached to the outside wall is really getting on my nerves.

I dab a bead of sweat from my brow with my napkin. I turn my head left and right, try to see if she's coming. I'm able to make out the corner bakery from where Emma and I grabbed pastries while looking further down the cobbled street towards a junction.

Alice turns the corner. She makes her way towards me through a thin crisscrossing crowd. She's dressed casually. A flowing white blouse. Birkenstock sandals. A pair of Aviator sunglasses. Her dirty-blonde hair has been styled and chopped into a pixie cut, her fringe swept to one side.

I realise how much she blends into these surroundings. The same complexion, same manner as the locals. The same relaxed posture.

"That's a pretty drastic change," I say, eyeing her new haircut as she takes a seat opposite me. "What brought that on?"

She ignores the question. "Why do you want to see me like this?"

A waiter comes over to take her order. She responds in the native language. The two share a joke and laugh.

Her smile fades though as the waiter turns back inside the café and her attention returns to me.

"So what's this about, Luke?"

I let out a long sigh. "I need your help."

"With what?"

"I need you to help me leave."

"The club?"

"Yeah. I need you to help get me off this island. I need you to help me get my passport back."

The waiter sets a cappuccino in front of her. She asks him for something else and they exchange another joke. The waiter laughs a lot harder this time.

She stirs the cappuccino foam, waits for the waiter to leave before answering me.

She takes a sip of her coffee and then looks at me. A sympathetic smile momentarily crosses her lips. "And how exactly do you think I can help you with that?"

A pain au chocolat is placed in front of her. She takes a bite and chews, keeping her gaze fixed on me.

"Well, I know what's going on," I respond, the words in my head not forming as quickly as I would like. "The drug runs… the tensions on this island… the trouble over in South America. I can't do this, Alice. I don't have it in me. I just can't do it. I want to go home."

"So you had no issue with dealing, no issue with cutting with your best buddy and taking whatever you wanted in the process," she replies between mouthfuls. "But you want to bail now something more is expected of you? You've got a sense of what's going on and you don't like it? Is that right?"

I shrug and shake my head, eyes fixed to the ground.

"I guess," I say, my voice trailing off.

"I see," she nods, taking another mouthful of coffee. "Let me see if I've got this right, Luke. Because I'd hate to misinterpret you, or take your words out of context. I want to be completely fair to you here." She pauses. "Okay, first of all, you thought you'd have a cool summer working in a club, right? One non-stop party. Then you realised that you'd have to push some drugs, but that didn't bother you in the slightest. Victimless crime, make some extra cash, that kind of thing. No harm if some kids get off their tits on a summer blowout. But now something more is expected of you. And you don't like it. You're worried about what could happen to you. So you think now's a good time to leave. Have I got all of that right?"

My face reddens. "Yeah. I guess so."

"Kind of like being happy to eat the hamburger but not wanting to kill the cow, don't you think?"

"Hang on, Alice," I say, lifting a hand to stop her. "That's out of order. How was I supposed to know that I'd be expected to risk my life in fucking South America at some point, when K-OS and Lucio first took me on? That wasn't what I signed up for here."

"So K-OS didn't give that whole 'nothing comes for free out here' spiel?"

I say nothing, look past her in the direction of the corner bakery.

"Exactly," she responds. "Don't kid yourself thinking you were the first to get that talk. It's almost as old as time itself. Hell, he even gave it to me back in the day. He's right in what he says. Nothing he offers comes for free out here. Everyone has to pay him back eventually."

Silence.

Background chatter. String recording. The clack of plates being stacked.

"I'll even bet he mentioned Neverland," Alice says. "You know—Peter Pan and Tinkerbell?"

"He did. Said it was like Neverland out here."

"And what was the trade-off in Peter Pan? What did the Lost Boys give up, Luke? Think about it. Their very humanity. Never experience love, heartbreak, self-growth. Never mature. Never start a family. Never become a fully rounded person. All in order to stay a child forever at someone else's mercy. Don't you think that's pretty dark when it's put as bluntly as that? Without the Disney gloss applied?"

I shake my head.

She continues. "Well, it's exactly like that, you see. That's the trade-off. You live out here completely in the moment but with no scope for anything else. Seems like a pretty sweet deal. A great escape. That is until you realise that even the Lost Boys had to occasionally fight Captain Hook."

She breaks to gulp back the last of her coffee. I've still got around three-quarters of mine sitting cold in the cup.

"And it's the same out here, Luke. It feels win-win at first. No downside at all. Party after party after party. Non-stop. Drink what you want. Take what you want. Fuck who you want. The best parts of your teenage years repeated day after day for as far as you can see into the future. But you and almost everyone else thinks there's no catch, for some reason. You listen to K-OS talk about nothing good coming for free, and figure he's just talking for the sake of it. Pretty fucking naïve, don't you think?"

She stops again, looks around and exhales in a long, drawn-out fashion.

"I don't know what to tell you, Luke. I don't know how I can help you. No offence, but you're pretty misguided if you think I had it in me to wave a magic wand. Convince Lucio to release your passport so you could go ahead and book a flight home after a shake of the hand and a big pat on the back for your efforts. It doesn't work like that, Luke."

A tear rolls down my cheek. I bury my head in my hands.

"I—just thought you'd help me out—"

"Why? Because I'm nice to you? Because I've given you lifts home in the past? God knows I've needed someone at work to talk to, Luke, because everyone else patently hates my guts. It's not a nice position to find yourself in, you know. Everyone else at the club thinks I'm some fucking unemotional ice maiden, the teacher's pet, just because I'm fucking Lucio. Forgive me if I just wanted to show that I'm not the person people think I am. Can I not just do something nice without someone thinking I can do them a favour? It's the same handing out fucking flyers outside the club. I make eye contact with boys and talk to them, even laugh at their dumb jokes and occasionally come over all tactile, and they think that's a way in." She shakes her head. A cutting smile. "You remember that, Luke? You know exactly what I'm talking about, don't you? Why the hell is it that whenever I drop my guard or try to be nice, people think they can take advantage? It's fucking bullshit."

The tuneless string music plugs the silence.

"But I suppose you can establish why I put those barriers up, huh, Luke? It doesn't really take a genius to see why I can be cold as ice ninety-nine per cent of the time, huh?" She folds her arms, leans forward across the table. "Because I have to do what's best for me, Luke. I have to in order to survive. Because I can't even bring myself to think about the alternative. Ever since I realised what I had got myself into when I started working at the club, I've had to do whatever I can in order to stay one step ahead of things. Every fucking morning when I wake up and every night when I go to bed, all of this goes through my mind. I have to think what I can do next. I have to have a sense of how things are going down, even before most people get a feeling that there's something wrong. And do you know what, Luke? It is so fucking exhausting. It's hard enough doing all of this just for me without having to keep an eye on somebody else."

She pauses for breath, flicks some crumbs from the pain au chocolat around the plate.

"So if being thought of as some heartless bitch, some opportunistic snake, is a small price to pay for survival and staying ahead of the game, then so be it. But I'm sure you'll excuse me for feeling vulnerable just once and reaching out to someone. If only to show that there actually is blood pumping through my veins. That I'm not such a bad person."

We order another round of drinks. Alice asks for an espresso. I order a Fanta Lemon.

The waiter sets our drinks down in front of us during a pregnant silence.

"Let me tell you a story, Luke," Alice says in a quiet voice. "Something that I think will help you understand what I mean when I talk about doing everything I can in order to survive."

She sighs heavily before beginning.

"I came out here about six or seven years ago. Pretty similar circumstances to yourself. To most people who come out here, in fact. A holiday abroad with their friends. A summer blow-out after a year of uni. A break from work. An escape from the real world. A chance to reinvent myself, if only for a week. You know how it is, Luke."

She stirs the espresso.

"I had a lot of hang-ups back then. I was having a tough time at university. I wasn't enjoying it at all. I felt like I didn't fit in, no matter how hard I tried. I was used to being popular at school—a big fish in a small pond and all that—so to go from that environment to one in which you're essentially a nobody and everything feels so new and overwhelming... I found it all too much. I missed my friends from home. I missed my family. I was living miles away in a city that I just couldn't take to. The girls I lived with in student digs were nice enough, but they weren't my friends—if that makes sense? Our experiences were completely different. And I think it's impossible to ever truly bond with someone if there's no shared perspective of the world. They were city girls who were interested in—or at least pretending to be interested in—all this artsy shit which just went over my head. French cinema. Russian literature. That kind of stuff. I was a girl from a small town who liked MDMA, vodka and boys. That was about it. None of the things they were into meant anything to me. If you asked me who fucking Godard and Dostoevsky were, I'd have probably said they played at the last World Cup or something."

I laugh.

She allows herself a self-deprecating smile.

"Don't get me wrong, I'm not an idiot. I refuse to have people think I'm a bimbo or some sort of small-town hick. I could talk anybody under the table when it comes to politics and economics. They're interests which came much later on, obviously. I can talk about The Prince until the fucking cows come home, Luke. It's just that all of that pretentious stuff was never my scene back then. It didn't do anything for me, and I had never met anyone in my life who talked about the kind of stuff those girls did. Maybe I was a little bit naïve in thinking I could fit in without doing my homework. It's as if those girls had spent years honing an image that they knew would help them fit in at university, whereas I was basically turning up thinking I would just slot in the same way I did back home with my old friends."

She throws back the espresso in one mouthful.

"Anyway, I was pretty miserable. I wasn't enjoying the university life, and that was impacting on my studies. I just about scraped through the first year, but I really struggled beyond that. I lost interest. I was basically burning through my student loan and maxing out the student credit card I got because I simply didn't give a shit. I was running up huge debts going out and taking all sorts, because I figured I may as well get something out of the lifestyle they make a big deal of promoting. I just didn't care how it was being funded or who was paying for it, because why would I? Kids don't really give a shit about that kind of thing, do they?"

She looks beyond me for a moment at the inside of the café.

The Heat of the Summer

"So when my friends from back home got in touch and said they were organising a holiday abroad, I didn't need to be asked twice. I just went along with it without a moment's thought. I couldn't have given a crap about anything else. The notion of being away with my girls, falling back into my old role, was like heaven. It was exactly what I needed. Of course, some of it went on the credit card and the rest was courtesy of the Bank of Mum and Dad. I don't think they were especially happy about that because they were getting a sense that I was really frivolous with money and that I wasn't applying myself to my studies. They were right, of course. They were really worried that I was going off the rails. And whenever they broached the subject on the phone I either snapped at them or just hung up. My relationship with them really plummeted. And it's never really picked up after everything that's happened since. I don't think it's a stretch to say that they consider me a disappointment. At my age right now, they probably envisaged that I'd have a steady job and one foot on the property ladder, looking to settle down with a nice guy and start a family rather than hand flyers and sell drugs to fucked-up tourists outside a nightclub thousands of miles away. I can't really blame them when it's put that way, I suppose."

"When did you last see your parents?"

She shrugs. "Years ago. They flew out here and met Lucio and that was it. I don't think they were too impressed seeing what I do for a living and the company I keep. I think it's preferable for them to pretend that I don't exist. I can't even recall the last time we spoke on the phone. They may as well be a couple of strangers now."

"So that's why you stayed out here? You met Lucio?"

She shakes her head and bites her bottom lip. "No, not exactly. It was K-OS at first."

"You were with K-OS?" I manage, shocked.

"Yeah. For a little bit. I was having such a great time out here. It was a literal escape from my life. I know I make it sound like I didn't give a shit about anything at the time, but my general attitude was clearly a way of coping with how unhappy I was. If I felt like I didn't care about what I was doing, how much money I was spending, then it became easy for me to push it to the back of my mind. I hung out at Pandemonium a lot on that holiday. K-OS was DJ-ing, even then. I was already going over the idea of staying out here because I simply didn't give a fuck about anyone or anything back home. I figured I could start a new life and have some fun. I couldn't go back to the past so I thought I may as well make a future on my own terms. Fuck everything else. That was my thinking at the time."

"So you got with K-OS?"

"I think he had started noticing me at the club. I made a move at one of the boat parties and that was it, really. We started hanging out and going to parties together and he introduced me to a pretty cool crowd. And obviously we got fucked together a lot of the time. Freebies that were a real nice perk. Towards the end of the holiday, he asked me to stick around. He said he didn't want me to leave. And I already had it in my head that I wanted to stay anyway. I would have done even if he hadn't asked, but that just sealed it. Made it even clearer in my own mind that I was doing the right thing."

"So what happened next?"

"Well, we were a couple, to all intents and purposes. On the surface at least. But things were pretty volatile. It's not the kind of thing I expect any sympathy for because we were both as bad as each other. We spent most of our time together either fucking or getting off our tits. It's hardly the kind of dynamic which makes for a healthy, harmonious relationship. He was even fucking other girls from the club—tourists and shit—but that never really bothered me all that much. I happily turned a blind eye to all that sort of stuff because I was still getting free coke at the end of the day. He could have been fucking the Pope and I couldn't have given any less of a shit."

She runs her hands through her hair, gathers her thoughts.

"But then I obviously learned what you have, Luke. I realised that I was being prepped for a tour to the other side of the world. K had moved on to other girls and the pretence of a relationship had all but ended. I was just a fucking toy for him. He was using me the same way I used him as a way into this world. And this is what he means when he talks about nothing coming for free. He extended his hand and I took it. The time had come when I had to give something back. And like you, I was scared at the prospect. I told him I didn't want to. He hit me a couple of times. Beat me up really bad. The kind of beating that forced me to take a week or two off work because the bruises were that violent, no amount of make-up could hide them. And that's when I turned to Lucio."

"And then what?"

"I just threw myself at his feet. I fawned over him. I followed his every move and hung on his every word. I made myself completely available to him. Surrendered myself. I left one and focused on the other. See, K-OS and Lucio's relationship is strictly professional. There's no friendship there. No real loyalty. Both just do what's best for business. Lucio has the land and the property and the contacts, K-OS has the influence and the means of distribution. No doubt there's tension there because Lucio has had to warn K about getting high on the supply a couple of times, but that seems to be under control now. It's a pretty solid set-up on the whole. Anyway, I figured that if I aligned myself with Lucio, there would be no way in hell he'd allow me to go to South America and face all the dangers that come with the trip. And that's precisely what happened."

"And what about K-OS?" I ask. "How did he respond to it?"

Alice shrugs, catches a tear on her cheek. "In his usual manner. He still gives me a hard time and treats me like shit. But like he is with Lucio, our relationship is strictly professional. We both have jobs to do. We try not to let our feelings or our past get in the way. We put on our game faces for any new starters, present a united front and all of that shit."

"Does Lucio treat you better?"

"Not really the point of what I'm trying to say, is it, Luke? The most important thing is that I'm in a secure place at the minute. There's so much shit that's out of my remit. I don't have to deal with K to the extent that you and the other workers do. If I have to feign interest in Lucio or fuck him a couple of times a week to keep things that way, I'll happily put up with it. If he's distant or distracted and pays me no attention for days at a time or goes off to fuck some other women, then I'll put up with that, too. I'll put up with almost anything, do almost anything as long as it keeps me safe from harm. But, you see, Luke, if I were to swipe your passport for you, I'd be jeopardising my position of privilege. Lucio doesn't slap me around as much or as hard as K-OS did, but you can guarantee he'd fucking kill me as soon as look at me if he noticed that a passport was gone and suspected I had something to do with it."

Alice gets a hold of herself again. She furrows her brow, puts on a stern face. She clasps her hands together and makes eye contact.

"So, Luke," she resumes. "Considering all of that, why exactly should I help you out when nobody ever afforded me the same courtesy? When nobody warned me what I was getting into? Why should I take on more work when looking after myself is hard enough?"

A terse silence.

Music and chatter blend in the background.

I look away from her, down at the ground.

"Because I've killed someone."

Her eyes widen. "You've what?"

"I've killed someone," I repeat softly.

She shakes her head. "How? Who?"

"I don't know. Some kid. I think he was selling stuff in the club. K-OS was holding him captive somewhere up in the mountains. He came round to my flat in the middle of the night and drove me up there. The kid was pretty beaten up and looked emaciated. I've never seen fear like what was etched on his face, I swear..."

I pause. The sentence trails to nothing. I take a breath, force myself to continue.

"...K-OS started cutting him up. He made me film it all on his phone. And then he gave me a gun and got me to put it inside the kid's mouth and then pull the trigger and..."

I stop again, my voice cracking as the words run away from me. My eyes start to fill with tears again and I run my hands down over my cheeks.

"K-OS was talking about sending a message. He's been saying stuff like that for a while. And Kevin told me about some turf war heating up over here with some rivals. Some guy called Teardrop. And..."

That's all I can manage before getting choked up.

I sight Alice through my tears. She's staring into space, her face set in a haunted expression. She eventually shakes her head and mutters something to herself.

Her voice then picks up. "Oh no. Oh no," she repeats. She stops to cover her face. "This is bad. This is really fucking bad."

"What?"

She gets up, leaves the table. "Luke, I'm really sorry, but I'm going to have to go."

"What? Where?"

"This is bad," she says again. "I... I need to speak to someone. Tell them about this. This is really fucking bad. Luke, I'm so sorry, like I said, but I really need to go. This is really serious."

She keeps apologising as she turns her back, weaving awkwardly between tables while tapping her phone.

27

The nights pass by, blurring together in a nightmarish sequence.
More outsiders push product in the club.
Fewer tourists frequent the Strip.
More parties in the apartment complex. Noise from indeterminate locations assaults me from every direction.
More inflatables punctured at sea. Dinghies. Rafts. Even lilos. More bodies washed ashore. Either reported as unfortunate boating accidents or deaths by misadventure. According to the rumours circling the club.
K-OS stalks and prowls Pandemonium. Stalks and prowls his penthouse. Broods in silence.
The heat intensifies day by day. A second wave at the very end of summer.
It's too hot to catch a breath. Bodies wilt, seeking respite in the shade.

———

Grandad's diagnosis was the final straw for me. Everyone has a breaking point and that was mine.

Ruby's death is something that I've learned to live with, now. That's not to say that it gets any easier, but that I've accepted it. That I know I'll carry it around with me until the day I die. It's just the way it is. I try not to think too much about it, even though it inevitably comes to mind every so often. Even then, I keep it to myself.

I took my parents' divorce in my stride. It's not exactly uncommon in this day and age, after all. I'm not the first kid who's gone through it. I won't be the last. If it's damaged me in any way, then there'll be untold scores of kids bearing the exact same scars. That's just a fact. Forever is much easier to swear to at the altar than to actually go through with. I get that. It's understandable to a degree.

Being estranged from my dad has bothered me less as time has moved on. Obviously, it was hard at first. You take it personally. But it soon became apparent that he wasn't a

The Heat of the Summer

nice person. I took little pleasure from his company as I got older. And, from speaking to my friends—can I even still call them that, after what's happened?—about their own dads and the problems they have, always butting heads and the like, I wonder whether conflict between father and son is something natural. I've listened to what the lads have said about fighting with their dads, and wonder whether I've simply been spared a lot of grief.

I've even grown used to the change in my mother. It's not been pleasant. She's damaged. Clearly still hurt. It doesn't take a genius to see. But it's understandable, like I've said. I've lived with her throughout it all and watched it happen. I've watched her become introverted and possessive. Spiteful and vindictive. Full of self-pity. She's been in a hole for a long time and I've not even tried to pull her out. I've simply learned to live with the person she's become because I've been struggling to keep a handle on things myself. I've been just about coping for the past decade now.

But something felt different when Grandad received his diagnosis. It felt like that was it. I couldn't keep going as I had. He was fit and healthy. Active and mentally sharp. It was implausible that he could receive such news. It felt like the cruellest practical joke imaginable. It just didn't make sense.

Grandad typically put a brave face on things. Tried his best to carry on as normal. But that has obviously become increasingly difficult as the weeks and months have gone by. The bad days outnumber the good now. The pills have less effect. The memory fails regularly. The middleweight-boxer frame that he had maintained since his youth and took great pride in has sunk and sagged. The last time I saw him, he was hunched over in the doorway of his granny flat, struggling to present his bag-of-bones body in any kind of positive light.

We're now at the stage where he has to be humoured a lot. It only causes him distress to be corrected about the things he is so adamant about.

He is effectively living in his own little shrinking world.

The diagnosis was the last thing I needed. I'd been through so much and there were so many things in the future that I found myself stressing over, constantly worrying without so much as a moment's respite, that it didn't seem fair to have to contend with this about Grandad.

When the lads asked me if I wanted to come away with them, I was in two minds.

That's actually being generous. I wasn't at all keen at first. The thought of being out of my comfort zone terrified me. I'm not an extrovert. I struggle to fit in with my surroundings the way it seems almost everyone else can. Switch off. Go with the flow. I've never been able to do that.

Visiting Grandad one day changed my mind about the holiday. It wasn't any words of wisdom as such, the kind he may have dispensed in the past. No advice based on past experience. It was the fact that he was like a zombie staring open-mouthed at the wall.

I put the kettle on and made us each a cup of tea. But my presence failed to register on Grandad's face. He was scruffily dressed in a dirty old white T-shirt that hung on him like excess skin and a pair of muddy jogging bottoms, as though he had been out in the garden. His hair was messy and he was unshaven. I set the cup of tea down in front of him and it took him a while to respond. Not even the noise of the blaring television could break the trance.

Grandad eventually became lucid as the tea was cooling in the mug. It took an age for him to turn his head towards me and offer a broken smile made all the more tragic by the white hair sprouting from his chin.

He asked me what my name was again.

It was hardly an unusual question under the circumstances. I had grown used to it. It no longer elicited the same crestfallen response from me as the first time he asked. Now only weary resignation.

I re-introduced myself and he came over apologetic, as he always did after such lapses. I knew the routine. He would blame the forgetfulness on tiredness, his pills—whatever came to mind first, ironically. His face would flash beetroot red and there would be a glimmer of his old self in a self-deprecating remark.

But there was little of that this time, aside from the initial apology. He simply returned to gazing dead ahead. The light from the TV danced across his pallid face. He clacked his tongue and lazily turned his head again and asked how Ruby was doing.

If she was well. If she was enjoying school.

I clenched my teeth, pushed back a sigh. The question poked the sadness inside me.

The flicker of a half-smile across my face hid my feelings. I managed an insipid "fine", which seemed to placate Grandad in that moment. He returned to gawping at the television, lost in his hazy, disjointed thoughts as though nothing had been said at all.

Call it fate or serendipity or whatever else, but The Wizard of Oz came on the television after the adverts had finished. It had been ages since I last saw it. Maybe only once or twice since turning thirteen.

I was surprised by how much of the film I remembered. I don't mean the iconic scenes, like Dorothy opening the door of the house into Oz or meeting the characters who accompanied her on the journey to Emerald City; more the sepia prelude featuring Aunt Em and Uncle Henry, Miss Gulch and Professor Marvel. I'm talking about the dialogue and the plot points from this portion of the film that virtually nobody thinks about. The boring stuff, if you want to sound crude. It affirmed to me how cruel, how boring, how utterly unfair ordinary life can be.

I was still shaken by my grandfather's question about Ruby.

The fact that it was uttered so innocently by somebody who was gradually becoming a stranger only compounded matters. It broke my heart. Reiterated that the person I knew and loved was slipping away.

The Heat of the Summer

None of it seemed fair. I had no idea why things couldn't have just stayed as they were. Whenever things moved on, whenever things changed, it was invariably for the worst. And, sitting on the couch that day, I felt like I was just about done with everything.

I even thought about my own future. About moving away. Starting university. They were things causing me a great deal of anxiety. The uncertainty of what was to come.

I didn't think it was a stretch to assume that it would be another change that would only bring further unhappiness.

So that was when I made up my mind. At that moment, I decided to get away from everything. I had to escape. I was going to leave all of this behind, if only for a week. I closed my eyes and muttered under my breath that I was going to do it. Get everything out of my head.

A week away from reality. I figured it would be worth it.

—

Street lamps blink in the midnight darkness. "Show Me Love" by Robin S. plays low on the radio. The only other sound is the hum of the car engine left running.

Alice is in the driver's seat of the silver convertible. We're parked outside my apartment building. She stares straight ahead. Says nothing.

Eventually she turns the key to silence the engine. Low-playing dance beats drift out of the building through an open window and across the humid night-time air.

She clears her throat and addresses me without turning her head, without breaking her concentration.

She speaks slowly, icily. She tells me that things have changed since our previous meeting in the old town. The rules are different now. The means of survival have drastically altered.

She says that she can help me. But only if I help her.

I ask her how.

She says she will get my passport if I can do something for her. Then it's all on me to get home.

I ask her what she needs me to do.

The Heat of the Summer

The dance beats grow louder in the background.

She says she knows someone. Someone who managed to get into K-OS's penthouse one night. A friend, she is quick to add.

I ask her who.

She ignores the question. She draws breath, her hands running up and down the wheel before gripping it white-knuckled. She says this friend planted a gun. Planted it in a place K-OS would never even think to look.

"Where?"

"In the cistern of his toilet", she replies.

"And then what?"

I ask this despite knowing what comes next.

"It's all on you. You have to kill K-OS. It's all on you. You have to do it, Luke. It has to be you."

"Why?"

"Because he trusts you. You have a key to his place. You come and go as you like and he doesn't say a word. You're the one person he would never suspect of anything."

The air conditioning blows cool.

I tense up.

Some people from work enter the building. They don't see us. The car headlights are switched off.

A light goes on in one of the apartments.

"Do you just expect me to open fire? Like someone from an action film or something? Fucking Bruce Willis in Die Hard?"

Alice shrugs. "Do whatever you have to. You've used one before. I'm sure it'll come back to you. It must be like riding a bike."

I shake my head. "There's no need for that."

"Sorry. Poor attempt at humour," Alice replies in the same flat tone. "But you need to do this, Luke. You're the only person who can get in there without arousing suspicion. You do this and I'll get you your passport. No questions asked."

"But what about the police? They'll be looking for me."

The Heat of the Summer

"Don't worry about the police. Lucio knows people. They'll bury this along with K-OS. You'll be far away from here not too long after."

Silence.

More people stream into the building. More lights go on. Songs are played louder. The noise pounds my temples.

"So what happens if I fuck it up?"

She turns her head, glares at me.

"You'll die a whole lot quicker than if you decide not to go through with it at all."

28

K-OS and I cut in silence.

He's playing opera again. Wagner's "The Ring Cycle", he says.

The noise hurts my head. I can barely concentrate on what I'm doing.

Coke is stacked high on the glass table in front of us, along with the usual shit like ripped-open boxes of baking soda and laundry detergent.

I'm conscious that I'm working at a much slower pace than usual.

And I'm certain that K-OS has noted my speed—or lack of, rather—but I find myself praying that he doesn't suspect anything is the matter.

The air conditioning emits a quiet drone.

I'm staring straight ahead at the white wall, hoping that I'm only imagining seeing K-OS shooting long and dissatisfied looks at me out of the corner of my eye.

There's nothing projected in front of us tonight. Thankfully.

I could not have taken it.

I told K-OS I was feeling ill and that I didn't have the stomach for any gruesome films. He asked what was up. I said a temperature and a feeling of listlessness. I asked if I should go home, thinking I may contaminate the product, but he shrugged and said it's not like it matters much.

But he said he still wanted his opera on. He was insistent.

Right now I'm coughing and spluttering, hocking up phlegm, wiping my brow to the point where it's actually difficult to say for certain if I am genuinely ill, or if I've actually managed to convince myself that I am.

I catch a disgusted look from K-OS out of the corner of my eye.

"Do you mind if I use the bathroom, K?" I ask.

"I think you'd better," he growls.

I cough walking over to the bathroom partition.

The Heat of the Summer

"There are some painkillers in the cabinet above the sink," K-OS calls to me.

I look over my shoulder. "Are you sure you don't want me to just go home, K? I know you're not bothered about the product, but I wouldn't want you to get ill."

His laugh booms around the open space. "That shit is for mere mortals, kid. Trust me, I never get sick."

I run cold water in the sink. I splash some onto my face and wipe it on my forehead over my cheeks.

I stare at my reflection in the cabinet mirror. Bloodshot eyes. Tired skin. My worries on display.

I open the medicine cabinet and rummage behind deodorants and aftershaves for some painkillers. A glint from a small wire basket on the bottom shelf catches my eye. I shift a couple of packets of tablets and toothpaste tubes. Reach inside. Pull out a gold tooth.

I drop it as soon as the realisation hits.

An image of Ryan enters my head.

The tooth falls into the water, sinks to the bottom of the basin. I fish it out, dry it with the hem of my T-shirt and try to stop my hands from shaking while carefully placing it back inside the basket. The exact same place as before. Stack the tablets and the toothpaste tubes on top.

But the basket still holds my attention.

I reach for it a second time. I toss out the pills and the toothpaste tubes again and sift through to the very bottom. A few scored pale patches with the consistency of leather. What I think is an ear lobe. Part of a cheek. Each one is around a square inch in size, jagged with red specks decoratively streaked.

There are ear studs. Chokers. Rings. Even a wrist watch.

Two Ibuprofen tablets are out on the sink beside the cold tap that I must have cracked from the packet without realising. I throw them into my mouth and wash them down with water I scoop from the basin, then splash some more over my face.

I put everything away. Close the medicine cabinet door.

I pull the plug from the basin and move over towards the toilet. I drop my trousers, force out a shit and then wipe my arse. Pretend that I haven't noticed the blood on the paper.

Back over to the sink. I sort myself out. Pull myself together, washing my hands.

I glance over at the cistern. I suck in some air and close my eyes.

Try to picture doing what Alice wants.

I clasp my hands around the edge of the porcelain lid. Remove it from the cistern.

I peer inside.

Empty.

I rest the lid on the toilet seat, try to compose myself again and dip a hand inside the tank. Splash around for the feel of a gun.

But nothing comes.

I move the cistern lid back in place and sit myself down on the toilet seat and pull my knees in close to my chest, then move my hands over my face and begin weeping uncontrollably, no longer able to keep a lid on everything churning deep inside me.

There's nothing left.

I just want to go home now. I want this all to end.

I slide open the access panel to leave the bathroom.

K-OS is standing on the other side. He grabs me by the throat and forces me against the partition.

"The fuck you been doing in here, kid?" he scowls.

"K— K—" I wheeze.

"Have you been fucking snooping? You've been gone a while, kid. That must have been some almighty shit, boy."

A rasp is forced from my throat. He pushes my head back against the wall.

The taste of blood in my mouth. A warm strand of sick dribbles down my chin.

".... please..."

K-OS releases his grip. I collapse to the floor, heaving. A series of hard coughs. Gasps. I drag myself on my hands and knees across the cold tiled floor towards the toilet, and puke out my guts.

K-OS's footsteps draw close. He grabs the hair around the back of my head, pulls tight.

I yelp.

"You sound like a bitch," he spits.

I heave inside the toilet bowl. The coldness stings my cheeks. The smell of bleach burns inside my nose.

"K—" I start.

He pushes my head to the bottom. Gargled cries. Bubbles rise to the water's surface.

He jerks me back. Slaps my cheeks.

Relieved breaths.

K-OS then squats on his haunches, lowers his head to mine. "So what have you been getting up to in here, kid?" he asks. "Snooping? Planting something? Has someone else got to you? Had a word in your ear?"

"K, I swear…" I pant. Air and words both come difficult. "I… I don't know what you're talking about. I'm sick, K. I was just trying to get my head together. That's all."

"You swear? You fucking swear?"

"Yes, K, yes."

He slaps the back of my head and stands upright, looms over me. He grabs a bottle of bleach from beside the toilet. He unscrews the cap, thrusts the bottle in front of me.

"When you said a bad word as a kid, did your mother ever threaten to wash your mouth out with soap?"

I nod.

I run my hand over the ache at the back of my head. Blood on my fingertips.

K-OS goes on. "Classic trick, huh? I think they must have taught every new mother that one at the hospital. They must hand out pamphlets on how to discipline your kids or something. Only my mother, you see, she had a bit of a screw loose. She always had to go one step further. She never liked to be outdone by anybody."

The Heat of the Summer

He stops for a moment. Smiles. Allows a dry laugh to leave his throat.

"It must have been exhausting being that woman, now I think about it. Being a black woman in a white man's world. Always feeling you have to prove something to everybody. But I suppose it worked for me and my little sis, growing up. Me, in particular—well, I don't mind admitting that I was scared stiff of my mother. See, I was a model child because of that. That probably surprises you, doesn't it, kid? But, yeah, I wouldn't have said boo to a goose as a kid. I even stepped one millimetre out of line and that was it. And that woman sure could give a beating and then some, believe me."

He stops and lifts the back of his hand. Laughs a second time.

"But, anyway, that side of my mother's personality—I guess she must have passed it on to me because, as you know, kid, I am certainly not one to be trifled with or made to look like a fool. I am not one to be outdone on any score. If you can inspire fear, then people eat out of your hands even if you only give them crumbs. No-one will even think about trying to take you on. If I learnt anything from her or if anything at all was passed on, it was that same ruthless streak."

K-OS screws up his face, studying me. His lips twist in a half-smile.

"Trust me, I'm going somewhere with this," he says. "The point I'm trying to make is that your parents fuck you up, as that racist motherfucker Larkin once said. A very, very astute observation. Credit where it's due. Anyway, my mother didn't stop at the old 'soap in the mouth for bad language' threat. She was a God-fearing woman of good Ghanaian stock. She fretted about my soul so much that she took that shit one step further. What if she got wind that a lie had left my lips? She didn't want her little boy burning in hell for all eternity. So she thought that a logical next step was bleach in the mouth. Cleanse my tongue for having dared to speak ill. She figured it would be better for me to spend a night in hospital than forever at Satan's side. But, either way, she never had to spend that night in hospital praying for the Lord to give me a second chance because just the threat itself was more than enough for me. I was straight as an arrow for that woman."

He pauses abruptly, looks at me square through his sunglasses. He reaches out and pinches my nose to force open my mouth. He shoves the open bottle barely an inch from my tongue.

"Now, kid, I wonder if the threat alone is enough for you. I think a lot of you, you know. And I want to believe you. Do you swear to me you aren't lying?"

I shake my head hard. "No, no, I swear, K," I cry out in an obstructed voice. "I'm ill. I just needed a break. That's all. I wasn't up to anything, I swear."

He relaxes his fingers from my nose. I gasp for air and fall forwards, pushing out my palms for support. I spit on the floor. I then look up to apologise to K-OS through a fit of tears.

K-OS ruffles my hair. He screws the cap back on the bottle of bleach and puts it back beside the toilet.

I keep my eyes fixed to the floor. Feel K-OS's disdainful look burn.

"Loyalty and respect, kid," he says. "That is all I ask now and forever. You can manage that, can't you?"

I give a slow nod of the head, still gazing at the floor.

"And you'd never ever even think of lying to me, would you, kid?"

"No," I mutter.

He slaps my back. I crash to the floor. Collapse on my front.

K-OS steps out of the bathroom. "That's exactly what I wanted to hear, kid," his voice reverberates through the open door. "Like I've always said, everything is about sending a message. And then making sure it's received loud and clear."

29

I've hardly left my bedroom in days. Barely left my bed.

I've been fortunate in how my shifts have fallen. I was due some time off anyway. And I've called in sick for the past couple of nights.

K-OS has been WhatsApping me. Asking if I'm okay. Wishing me a quick recovery.

I've responded in appreciative terms without giving too much away. Made sure that my messages are short and straight to the point.

I'm trying to keep my distance.

It's been the only contact I've had with anyone from Pandemonium, Alice included. She's gone AWOL since I failed to do what she asked.

No messages. No calls. Nothing at all.

Noises from Kevin come through the walls. Blasts of video games. Loud music. Fucking noises from his bedroom. Not once has he come in my room to check on me. But I haven't been desperate for his or anyone else's company either.

I sometimes think about the gold tooth I found in K-OS's bathroom cabinet.

I think about Ryan.

And then I usually feel sick. So I try my hardest to push such thoughts from my mind.

Parties continue. Noise comes through the ceiling. Rises through the floorboards. Pounding beats and constant chatter. Wild cackles and snapping bedsprings.

A soundtrack playing from dawn until dusk.

My mind weighs heavy with all of this. There's a permanent throb between my temples, as though my head could split in two.

I return to my room after taking a shower. Kevin made a few cracks about me finally leaving my pit. Said something about kidding myself that I could escape my destiny out in South America. That there are usually a few good movies on the plane and the food out there is pretty good. All of this while taking tokes of a spliff, blasting people away on Call of Duty.

I pretend not to hear him. Don't give him the satisfaction of a response, even though the joke cuts pretty deep and I'm now at the point where I find myself thinking that I would probably rather die than spend another night on this island.

I wonder if I could go through with it. Maybe. I don't know.

—

I check my phone. A text message from an unknown number:

Don't go to the club tonight. Whatever you do. Just don't.

I call the number. It rings out.

I text something back. Asking who it is. Even though I know I won't get an answer.

I call in sick again and go back to bed.

The party noises continue around me.

I drift in and out of a fitful half-sleep. End up staring at the ceiling for the most part.

It's a little after midnight when Kevin barges into my room.

I'm considering a wank. My dick rock hard. The unexpected sight of him bursting through my door causes me to pull the covers and roll onto my side.

"Was I interrupting something?" Kevin smirks.

"For fuck's sake, Kev, I can't be arsed with this. I've got a splitting headache."

"Charming."

"What the fuck do you want?"

He takes a few steps towards me, holds out his phone. He sits down next to me on the bed.

"Have you seen what's happened at the club?"

"No."

The beam from the bedside lamp reveals a worried expression on Kevin's face.

I shuffle upright against the headboard.

He angles his phone close to me, his thumb hovering above the "play" function on a video.

"You need to see this, mate," he says.

The video is out of focus. Faces and limbs are blurry, barely distinguishable from each other, blending together. It's unmistakably Pandemonium. Given away by the confined space and the marble pillars across the pit and the fuzzy snippets of people dressed in work uniforms. The club itself appears half-full. The chorus to "Cola" by CamelPhat is audible over a dense collective chatter.

The camera jerks. Shows the bar. The pit. The DJ podium. A glimpse of the guy who occasionally fills in for K-OS spinning the decks. The entrance tunnel. The sudden formation of a bottleneck.

There's a series of loud bangs. Screams immediately follow, meshing with the music.

A hard zoom. The bottleneck. The picture comes into focus for the first time. Bodies clamber over each other to escape the club. Even those dressed in the Pandemonium uniforms. A mass panic. Elbows. Jostling. Fear scored across faces.

A sudden break in the swell. People disperse to all four corners. Louder screams. Cries for help.

A figure emerges from the tunnel. The motorcycle courier. Face covered by his helmet. The gym bag full of cash is slung over his shoulder, his left hand gripping the strap. The courier's right hand is wrapped around a gun. He points it towards the ceiling. Unloads. Walks in the direction of the bar. Marble and plaster raining down.

The camera's focus fluctuates. A high-pitched scream from the person filming. Pleas to God.

There's a final shot of the courier trudging down the corridor behind the bar and towards the office. A sight visible over the surge of revellers and club workers.

Cut to black.

Kevin pockets his phone. Looks at me wide-eyed, totally pale.

"What the fuck?" I ask.

Kevin shakes his head. "This is bad."

"What do you think is going on?"

He shakes his head a second time, runs his hands back through his hair and blows his cheeks.

"I don't know, mate," he responds, quaking. "I don't know."

"Have you spoken to anybody at the club?"

"I can't get through. And nobody has answered my texts."

"Shit."

Kevin nods. A grim look. "I think this is a reaction, you know."

Silence weighs heavy.

"K-OS," Kevin starts. "This is definitely a strike against him. No doubt about it. All of the shit he's been pulling recently. The expansion. Treading on other people's toes. No way was somebody like Teardrop ever going to let it slide."

The thought of telling him about the poor kid in the stone shack up in the mountains crosses my mind. My mouth opens, ready to speak, but nothing comes. Dead air.

Kevin picks up. "This is only going to get worse. K-OS is going to respond. Then these guys will do something back. It will just go on and on. It's all out in the open now. Guerrilla warfare. Blood will fucking run down the Strip, I'm telling you, man. There are clearly no rules anymore. Out of the window. Nothing off limits. And trust me, we're all fair game here, Luke. Every single one of us."

I try to call Alice.

No answer.

I text her several times.

Each message fails to send.

I slip out of the flat as Kevin flits between rooms packing his suitcase.

I suspect he won't even notice I've left.

I'm not even sure whether this is a good idea. But I feel I ought to do something.

Something that would at least reassure me that Alice is okay. For my own peace of mind.
—

The Strip is dead. Understandable why. Disconcerting nonetheless. Faint beats from faraway parties linger. Distant sirens. Forlorn neon blinks. The warm night-time air pinches my skin as I move through this eerie scene. A sickness rises in my stomach the closer I get to Pandemonium.

I step into the long shadow cast by the club. The grounds are deserted. A large alley cat creeping across a puddle of light is the only sign of life. The totemic building broods under a blanket of silence, emits a distinct unease.

I look up and down Pandemonium. The lights are on inside K-OS's penthouse. The windows wide open. Thin white curtains billowing in the breeze.

The air in the tunnel is still thick with sweat. My mind travels back to the first time I walked down this tunnel. The night I was embarrassed about introducing my friends to Emma and there was a tightness in my chest that was exacerbated by every step through the darkness. The suffocation induced by the tapering walls. "Panic Room" playing at such a volume that it provoked a headache and made me think I could pass out at any moment.

This is what goes through my head during the descent. My eyes set on the mouth of the tunnel in the middle distance.

The club appears empty. No bodies in sight. Tables and stools overturned. Spilt drinks. Dust and debris. The massive speakers from the podium collapsed in a heap.

Glass crunches underfoot while I explore the scene. I move from the pit to the DJ booth and then over to the bar. I feel dents and grooves on every surface. Bullet holes.

The door of the back office swings on its hinges. I take a closer look inside the office. The safe has been left wide open. All of the money, gone. There's no indication that the door has been tampered with. Still intact. No sign of physical damage.

I can only guess somebody punched in the code. Knew exactly what they were doing.

30

I take the service lift up to the penthouse.

The familiar ping of the parting lift doors fades to silence. I tread across the cramped airlock and fumble in my pocket for my key and then snap the lock and push open the front door to a long, jarring creak.

The lights are off now. Every window still wide open. A draught cuts through the vast living space. The balcony doors at the far end are extended outwards, offering a glimpse of bright lights blinking in the dark.

I consider shouting his name. The thought enters my head, only for my whole body to tense.

I sight the length of the penthouse. The living area, deserted.

I move around the place.

Bathroom. Kitchen. Study. Each partition closed.

I start to wonder if K-OS is even here. Whether he got wind of what was going on downstairs and fled.

It's while considering this I see the glow of a lamp through the bedroom screen door, casting the silhouette of a figure lying on the bed.

A choked whimper from the other side of the partition.

I hesitate at first, but eventually slide the screen door open. K-OS is spread across the bed, tangled in blood-stained sheets. His head is pointed at the ceiling, right hand clasped around his chest. Each breath is long and drawn out.

He twists his neck to face me.

"Kid, it's good to see you."

It's only the second time I've seen him without his sunglasses. There's a hangdog look to his features, a helplessness displayed in his one good eye. He looks even older than he has in recent weeks. His face crinkles, sucking in pain. He shifts his right hand from his bare chest to reveal two bullet holes. His torso washed claret.

He beckons me closer. Squints. Coughs some bile.

The Heat of the Summer

"The prick got me, kid," he chokes. "He fucking got me, didn't he?"

"What happened, K? Who are you talking about?"

The mattress groans under his weight as he struggles to get comfortable.

"He fucking came in here. Let himself in. Key in the lock like he lived here. Shot me in the heart, fair and square. Nothing more to it."

"Who?"

"I thought—I thought it was the courier at first. The guy from the club. Ferries the product. Brings back the money. I thought—he had fucked me over. But then…"

His voice trails. Expression glazes for a moment.

"What, K?"

He shakes his head, takes a long look up at the ceiling. "He took off his helmet. And—and it was him."

"Who?"

"The face," he begins, fading before picking up again. "The face of vengeance."

"Come on, K. You can do this, man. Who was it?"

K-OS locks his eye on me as best he can, resists his drooping lid. "Him, kid. It was Him. The fucking Angel of Death. The Eater of Worlds. My fucking penance. All of it—rolled into one. He pulled that trigger and—and—I saw it all before my eyes. All of my misdemeanours. All my crimes. Taking more than I should have. Stepping on other people's toes. Moving in on their turf. All of it came back to me right there and then—hit home by those fucking hot pieces of lead."

He pauses. Draws breath.

"But tell me, kid. You didn't fuck me over, right? You swear you had nothing to do with this?"

I shake my head. "No, K. I swear. Promise."

He nods, spits some more bile across the sheets. "It must have been her. It had to have been. I was always worried she would fuck me over. I never trusted her to begin with. The fucking snake. All of this, gone. Because of her."

The Heat of the Summer

He looks back up at the ceiling. His chest contracts. His features droop. Only the hint of a smile, the corners of his mouth twisted slightly.

"Now, kid," he says in a low voice. "There is nothing left of this glorious city of temples and palaces."

Alice is all I can think about.

I need to know if she's okay. I need to know what this all means.

—

The white Chevrolet is the only vehicle in the private car park. I take K-OS's car keys from my pocket and climb inside.

I grip the wheel and close my eyes. Take a few minutes to calm myself.

I then turn to the sat-nav stuck to the windscreen, scroll through the contacts. I find Lucio's address. Hit the confirmation key.

The mechanised voice begins to relay the route, ordering me left out of the car park. "Hotel California" plays over the radio as my foot hits the clutch.

I shut the song off and begin the long drive in total silence, the roll of the tyres over tarmac the sole accompaniment.

—

Features of the drive have stuck in my head. The coastal road. The calm sea to my right. The patch of identikit stucco homes. The plush, leafy hill. The gated homes on either side.

The car climbs the plush, leafy hill. My foot eases off the accelerator as I approach the house.

The iron gates are open. I guide the car inside, park on the driveway.

I get out of the car and take a look around. The garage doors are shut.

I move to the front of the house. The door is open.

I pass through the sterile hallway. Step into the living area. The balcony doors are open, as they were when I was last here.

The Heat of the Summer

I try phoning Alice again. No reply, as expected.

I decide to check upstairs. I go back out to the hallway and climb the stairs up to a second floor comprising a long carpeted landing and framed impressionist artwork adorning cream-painted walls. Classical music plays somewhere. The sound of running water overlays the piece. There's a bathroom a few metres to my right, the door open an inch or so to allow steam to filter out.

I gently push the door. The music deafens me, coming from what I think is a speaker perched directly opposite me on a window sill. I wave away some dense bathroom mist and peer through.

A glass shower cubicle covered in condensation, the door of which is half-open. Glass panels completely shattered. A pool of blood at the foot of the cubicle stains the otherwise pristine white carpet. Lucio's naked body hangs out of the shower, slumped over the lip of the cubicle, surrounded by shards of glass. One side of his face, set in a hollow stare, is buried in the carpet. Blood trickles from his lips, combining with a much larger puddle seeping from the back of his head.

The music reaches a crescendo as my scream cuts in.

I leave the bathroom, fly down the landing and search inside every room in the hope of finding Alice.

One final call.

The line clicks dead.

31

I head back to the apartment simply because I don't know what else to do. Where else to go.

The journey back passes in a blur of my own confused thoughts. Nothing beyond the immediacy of the road ahead permeates the haze.

There's a heavy police presence at the bottom of the Strip. Cars parked on kerbs. Flashing blue lights. A yellow-taped cordon. Officers mill around the outside of Pandemonium clutching napkin-wrapped pastries and polystyrene cups of coffee, drifting between conversations with each other.

I park several blocks away. Not far from the old town. I take a slow walk along the deserted beach and move closer towards the sea so that the tide laps my trainers. I look out at what is in front of me, at the sea shimmering all the way out to the horizon. At the sun climbing ever higher in a cloudless blue sky.

The squawk of gulls overhead. The tide's constant hush.

The island is waking up. Another day like any other.

I unhook the key to K-OS's penthouse from my Rick & Morty keyring and hold it in my hand with his car keys. Close my eyes. Shut my eyes.

I throw them out to sea as far as I can. I then turn around and step back along the beach, concentrating on the noise of the waves and the seagulls so as not to hear a splash.

I call Mum. It rings out several times before going through to voicemail.

—

Hi Mum, I hope everything is okay back home. Look, I just want to say that I love you. If you get this message, then please give me a ring. If not, don't worry about it. Just pass on my love to Grandad. I love you, Mum. Bye.

—

I'm exhausted when I arrive back at the apartment complex. I can barely keep my eyes open. I hear the dying thuds of last night's parties all around me. Echoes through the floor and ceiling and corridor walls. Chilled beats. Obscured talk. Strained sex noises.

I walk down the corridor towards my flat in a daze. The floorboards moan and belly out under each step. The smell of damp is stronger than ever, curling the hairs inside my nostrils. Raw sewage baking under a hot sun. The cracked ceiling bulbs buzz and flicker. Cobwebs occupy the corners of door frames. Faded wallpaper peels off the walls.

None of this bothered me for a long time. I just got used to it. Simply got on with things.

And that was it.

I spot someone loitering at the opposite end of the corridor. A man. Tall. Heavily- built. He's dressed in boots and jeans and a zipped leather jacket, wearing a motorcycle helmet and holding what looks like a large brown envelope in his right hand. He turns sharply at the sound of my footsteps and strides towards me.

I look over my shoulder. The lift appears miles away. Barely a speck in the distance. I turn back around to see that the courier is just yards from me. I throw myself back against the wall and clasp my arms around my chest. My whole body convulses. I slide down the wall. Slump to the floor.

A shadow falls over me.

I bury my head in my arms, rock back and forth. "Please," I manage through tears.

The courier removes his helmet. A man in his late thirties with a leathery tanned complexion, jutting cheekbones and an angular chin and nose. His hair is neatly trimmed, barely half an inch long, with a thin greying ponytail draped over his shoulder. The dark tattooed outline of several teardrops runs from the inside edge of his right eye all the way down to the corner of his chapped anaemic lips.

He zeroes in with a cobalt stare. "You Luke?" he asks in a gruff voice. The hint of a foreign accent.

I nod, still hiding my face. "Yeah."

"Crystal's friend?"

I drop my hands.

The Heat of the Summer

"Is she okay?"

"She said this is for you."

He hands me a brown envelope. I rip it open, remove the contents.

A bundle of fifty-euro banknotes held together with an elastic band. My passport.

I drop the envelope. Thumb the passport to check it's legitimate. That it hasn't been tampered with. I make no attempt to count the money.

The guy speaks. "She said you helped us out. That this would be thanks enough."

"What?"

"She got the key to K-OS's place from you, didn't she?" he says. "She said you really helped us get that piece of shit. Give him what had been coming to him for a long time."

Maybe she took them without me realising. When my guard was down and I wasn't expecting it. Maybe when I was drunk or high or something. Maybe she broke into my room one night or pick-pocketed me when I was at work. I don't think I ever let the key out of my sight—out of my possession—this whole time. Not that I can recall.

But I just go along with what he says.

"Oh, yeah—yeah," I answer.

All of it is over my head. I suspect this guy knows it too.

"It's been a long and emotional night, kid," he says in a quiet voice. "But we won. That's the main thing. It's all over now."

I think about K-OS. I think about Lucio. The shots fired at the ceiling in the club late last night.

I can't pretend to know about the intricacies of this whole thing. A game I was never a part of. Far away from the table.

Perhaps it's for the best that I don't know. That I never know.

Perhaps it's for the best that I pretend that none of this ever happened to begin with.

I know it is, in fact.

"And it's over for you too now, kid. You've done your bit. There's more than enough cash in that envelope to get you home safe," the guy continues before heading back down the corridor.

I wait until he's close to the lift before calling him back.

He turns around. Glares.

It's a look which causes me some discomfort even from a distance.

"Alice," I start. "She's—she's okay, isn't she?"

"Who?"

"Sorry. Crystal," I say. "I meant Crystal."

The guy nods. "Yeah, she's cool. No need to worry about her. Trust me."

I give a tired nod. Stare into space.

The guy then calls back down the corridor again, hovering in the doorway of the open lift, one arm propped against the side. "Look, kid, I would get off this island ASAP if I was you. Not waste a second. Believe me, there are going to be some big changes around here."

32

Hi Mum.

How is everything? You and everyone else okay? ... Good. Good. You have no idea how happy I am to hear that.

Look, about that last voicemail ... Yeah, I know. It must have worried you sick. I honestly didn't mean to. It was just I was feeling a little blue and I knew that I hadn't spoken to you in a while, and— ... Mum, Mum, there is nothing wrong. Trust me. Everything's fine now. I promise.

But, anyway, Mum ... Look, I'm coming hom e... Toda y... Yeah, today. I'll be home late r... I know it's quite sudden, but it's just how things have worked out. Just one of those things, I suppose. I mean, I've obviously got university and I need to get my things packed and there's all of that other stuff I have to do, too. Do you think you can pick me up from the airport later, Mum? I'll text you my flight details when I get a chance ... Thanks, Mum. That's brilliant. I really appreciate it.

I've really missed you, you know, Mum. I can't wait to see you later. Give my love to everyone back home. I'll be seeing them soon enough.

I love you, Mum. Bye.

———

I visited Grandad the day before I left for my holiday. He was having another bad day.

I hadn't visited him as much as I should have. I'd found it far too upsetting. I hadn't spoken to anyone about how I felt. I don't know why. It was just easier to keep things to myself. I didn't know if anybody would understand.

And so I hid away instead. I made excuses whenever the subject of visiting him was raised by family members. My revision schedule and the exams obviously took precedence in people's minds but beyond that, I'd been a lot less busy than people thought. I made vague excuses about having to take care of various things for university. And they took my word for it.

The Heat of the Summer

I know it's cowardly, but I didn't have the heart to tell them what was going through my head the last few times I visited him. It's like he wasn't even my grandfather anymore. Just someone who looks like him. A shell of someone I loved. Barely a hint of the person I was so close to other than the occasional flicker of memory.

I'm not even sure if he knew who I was the last couple of times I visited. He didn't call me by name. I think he thought that I was some old friend he used to go drinking with back in his teens because he told me all of these stories about what they got up to, as though we were reminiscing. Dances. Concerts. Courting Nan. The things he used to get up to every weekend in his youth.

It took all my strength to smile and nod. To humour him. Implore him to continue when all I wanted was for him to shut up and return to watching the television in silence to spare us both the embarrassment. All he did was talk about the old days as though he was still living them in the present.

But then something strange happened. There came a brief moment of lucidity.

Grandad picked up the remote and flicked through the channels, finally settling on The Wizard of Oz, which was playing on one of the Sky movie channels. I can't recall whether the film sparked this re-emergence of who he was, or whether the clarity preceded him picking up the remote control. But I remember feeling a shiver as to how it all married up.

The Kansan cottage had landed in Munchkinland, killing the Wicked Witch of the East. Grandad then turned to me and remarked that my mother had told him that I was going on holiday with my friends.

He smiled. Took a mouthful of the tea I had poured for him. He swivelled to face me and told me to enjoy myself. To have the time of my life.

He said to make the most of it because it all passes so fast. In the blink of an eye.

And that was it.

The Heat of the Summer

The film played. His eyes turned glassy. His smile dulled. He glanced down at the floor and picked up his head to look far into the distance, his tongue lolling to one side.

—

I'm in the airport bar taking my time over a cold beer, trying as best as I can to relax. I take in my surroundings while occasionally glancing up at the departures board, waiting for my flight status to change.

It's a standard airport bar, really. Nothing much to describe. A few plastic tables and chairs scattered around a horseshoe-shaped serving hatch. There are a couple of middle-aged men in suits clutching tumblers of whiskey and ice, talking loudly to each other, arching their backs, laughing every so often. There are young couples and a smattering of hen and stag parties, all appearing dishevelled as though they can't get home quick enough. And there's a sad-looking woman in her early twenties sitting alone at a table, looking straight ahead, nursing a large glass of white wine, her fingers running up and down the stem.

I cast my eyes out of the giant floor-to-ceiling window. The sky has turned overcast. It's started to rain a little. I watch a plane as it ascends from the runway and disappears behind a clutch of grey clouds.

I lift the glass to my mouth and take a swallow of beer. I turn my head back to the departures board.

Boarding.

ACKNOWLEDGEMENTS

I would like to express my eternal gratitude to John Lake and Mick McCann from Armley Press for having belief in the book and for their guidance during the publishing process, in addition to having to put up with my pestering and inane questions.

I would also like to offer a special thanks to Daniel Jones, Chris Brown, Richard Fong and David Edgcomb for taking the time to read early drafts of the novel and provide honest and frank feedback. Every constructive comment--both positive and negative--was greatly appreciated and renewed my faith in the book during trying times.

Finally, I would like to thank the people who mean the most to me. The love and support my parents Sharon and Paul Randles have given me over the years has been extraordinary and I would not have been able to write this book without them. My partner Katie Redmond--the love of my life--has been a constant source of inspiration. She has undoubtedly made me both a better writer and a better person. The faith and belief she provides on a daily basis is nothing short of remarkable, and all of it is valued in ways I struggle to articulate. An extra special thanks also goes to my stepdaughter Isla Harrison for making me laugh several times a day with her quips, jokes and stories, and all of the impromptu wrestling bouts that reiterated the importance of taking a break and ended any thoughts I may have had about a career in UFC.

My most heartfelt apologies if there is anybody I have forgotten to include. Please know that if you have offered any form of support or encouragement over the years, it has meant the world and is appreciated in ways you can't imagine.

Twitter: @LRandlesWriter
Instagram: lrandleswriter

Other books from Armley Press

FICTION

In All Beginnings: Ray Brown
Whoosh!: Ray Brown
Thurso: P. James Callaghan
Stickleback: Mark Connors
Tom Tit and the Maniacs: Mark Connors
The Lost Boys of Prometheus City: A.J. Kirby
Hot Knife: John Lake
Blowback: John Lake
Speedbomb: John Lake
Amy and the Fox: John Lake
Before the Gulf: John Lake
Nailed: Mick McCann
Leeds, the Biography: A History of Leeds in Short Stories: Chris Nickson
The World is (Not) a Cold Dead Place: Nathan O'Hagan
Out of the City: Nathan O'Hagan
The Last Sane Man on Earth: Nathan O'Hagan
Reliability of Rope: Samantha Priestley
A Bad Winter: Samantha Priestley
Breaking Even: David Siddall
Fogbow and Glory: K.D. Thomas
Sex & Death and Other Stories: Ivor Tymchak
20 Stories High: Michael Yates
Dying is the Last Thing You Ever Want to Do: Michael Yates

NON-FICTION

Coming Out as a Bowie Fan in Leeds, Yorkshire, England: Mick McCann
How Leeds Changed the World: Encyclopaedia Leeds: Mick McCann

Find us at Facebook, Twitter, Amazon and armleypress.com

Lightning Source UK Ltd.
Milton Keynes UK
UKHW012353261022
411123UK00005B/91